Praise for *French R...*

'Beautifully written, superbly plotted ... at the end' *Daily Mail*

'The novel has Laurain's signature charm, but with the added edge of greater engagement with contemporary France' *Sunday Times*

'Anyone who enjoyed Laurain's previous novels *The President's Hat* and *The Red Notebook* will doubtlessly enjoy this new romp' *Portland Book Review*

'Witty, nostalgic – I was completely charmed' *Woman and Home*

'This gem blends soft humour and sadness with the extraordinary' *Sainsbury's Magazine*

'A tale of dashed dreams, lost love and rediscovered hope that is also an incisive state-of-the-nation snapshot' *The Lady*

Praise for *The Red Notebook*:

'This is in equal parts an offbeat romance, detective story and a clarion call for metropolitans to look after their neighbours ... Reading *The Red Notebook* is a little like finding a gem among the bric-a-brac in a local brocante' *The Telegraph*

'Definitely a heartwarming tale' *San Diego Book Review*

'Resist this novel if you can; it's the very quintessence of French romance' *The Times*

'Soaked in Parisian atmosphere, this lovely, clever, funny novel will have you rushing to the Eurostar post-haste ... A gem' *Daily Mail*

'An endearing love story written in beautifully poetic prose. It is an enthralling mystery about chasing the unknown, the nostalgia for what could have been, and most importantly, the persistence of curiosity' *San Francisco Book Review*

Praise for *The President's Hat*:

Waterstones Spring Book Club 2013 • Kindle Top 5 • ABA
Indies Introduce Choice • Shortlisted for the Typographical
Translation Award 2013

'A hymn to *la vie Parisienne* ... enjoy it for its fabulistic narrative, and the way it teeters pleasantly on the edge of Gallic whimsy' *The Guardian*

'Flawless ... a funny, clever, feel-good social satire with the page-turning quality of a great detective novel' Rosie Goldsmith

'A fable of romance and redemption' *The Telegraph*

'Part eccentric romance, part detective story ... this book makes perfect holiday reading' *The Lady*

'Its gentle satirical humor reminded me of Jacques Tati's classic films, and, no, you don't have to know French politics to enjoy this novel' *Library Journal*

Antoine Laurain was born in Paris, where he still lives. He wrote *The Portrait* while working as an assistant to an antiques dealer. He now writes full-time but continues to collect antiques. His award-winning novels include *The President's Hat*, *The Red Notebook* and *French Rhapsody*.

Jane Aitken is a publisher and translator from the French.

Emily Boyce is in-house translator and editor at Gallic Books.

The Portrait

The Portrait

Antoine Laurain

Translated from the French by
Jane Aitken and Emily Boyce

Gallic Books
London

A Gallic Book

First published in France as *Ailleurs si j'y suis*
by Les Éditions Le Passage, 2007
Copyright © Les Éditions Le Passage, 2007
English translation copyright © Gallic Books 2017

First published in Great Britain in 2017 by Gallic Books,
59 Ebury Street, London, SW1W 0NZ

A CIP record for this book is available from the British Library
ISBN 978-1-910477-43-4

Typeset in Fournier MT by Gallic Books
Printed in the UK by CPI (CR0 4TD)

2 4 6 8 10 9 7 5 3 1

Sic luceat lux

I.

THE MAN WHO LOVED OBJECTS

It sits at the bottom of a field: a windowless shed of corrugated iron a hundred metres square, with lights that stopped working some time ago. Each summer the metal walls heat up in the sun, making the temperature inside almost unbearable.

I could have hooked a lamp up to the electricity but I prefer candles. One by one I light twenty of them, which are arranged at random. Then I smoke a cigarette and pour myself a glass of whisky. It's a ritual. Behind an industrial-sized petrol can I keep an excellent Bowmore, still young. Like all great whiskies, its flavour has overtones of leather and peat, and its colour is light like chicken broth, not the amber of revolting bourbons. I drink it from a silver Louis XV mug that sits waiting for me on an old wooden workbench each time I visit. The metal walls have never been painted, but they have gradually rusted to that hue artists call burnt sienna. A brown so vibrant it is almost red.

I come here once or twice a month and spend a good two hours contemplating my collections, as I used to do in my study. I have many snuffboxes, some gold, some tortoiseshell, and wrought-iron keys decorated with dolphins or mythical beasts, glass paperweights with multicoloured patterns locked inside them, smelling-salts bottles made of the yellow fluorescent glass known as uranium glass, Dieppe carved-ivory virgins, *haute époque* ruby goblets and so many other objects. They are displayed on an old workshop table where I also have a cabinet with many compartments. I have stored various things in each of the twenty-four pigeonholes. It's a bit like those advent calendars I used to open as a child. There was a door for each day, and behind every door a little compartment containing a plastic toy. I went from day to day and from surprise to surprise right up to Christmas Eve when the real presents arrived.

All the presents I have given myself throughout my life as a collector are gathered here. It is my cabinet of curiosities, hidden from the prying eyes of others like secret rooms filled with fabulous objects should be, jealously guarded for their one true master. My cabinet of curiosities, tucked away as it is at the bottom of a farmer's field in the heart of Burgundy where there is no mobile phone signal, is particularly curious.

The summer heat is suffocating and the bales of hay that have been piled up to the roof of the shed for years and years are so dry that they could spontaneously combust at any moment. At the back, on the right, resting on bags of out-of-date fertiliser, is my portrait with its coat of arms.

Today I think I understand what really happened with that picture.

Now I sit down on the little rattan chair and, taking the first mouthful of whisky, ask the usual question, out loud. It makes me smile every time: 'Pierre-François Chaumont, are you there? Knock once for yes, twice for no.'

Then as I put my silver mug smartly down on the workbench, the ring of metal on wood produces the answer.

It all began a little more than a year ago. Far from Burgundy, in Paris.

It was late spring, and for several weeks I had been trying to make modest inroads into the living room. Bit by bit, over several years, my wife had succeeded in exiling my fabulous collections to one room of our apartment and now the 'study' was where all my treasures were stored. But I had recently broken through enemy lines in order to return a few Saint-Louis paperweights to the coffee table. Not long before, a terrible accident had seen a Baccarat crystal piece fall against the side of a bronze mortar and break clean in half. Two thousand euros up in smoke. The financial damage persuaded Charlotte to grant the remaining paperweights a safe haven. We agreed on the coffee table.

The following day, I fetched my matching burgundy Gallé vases with a moth motif and placed them either side of the fireplace, as my wife looked on disapprovingly.

'Break these and that'll be a hundred grand gone,' I told her, anticipating any snide remarks, and quoting the value in francs to ensure the already-inflated price tag had maximum effect.

The money argument clinched it, and I wondered what else I could claim was priceless and thereby bring back to the living room.

I had not bid for anything at Drouot Auction House for some time. Auctions are more intoxicating than any drink and, in contrast to a casino, even when you lose you still somehow feel like a winner: the money you had set aside for the lot you've missed out on is magically returned to your bank account; in your mind you had already spent it, so when you leave the auction house you feel richer than when you walked in. It sometimes seemed to me that I might do well to get myself barred from Drouot, the way some gamblers have themselves banned from casinos. I pictured a big, burly bouncer, dressed like the doorman of a luxury hotel, letting everyone past until he caught sight of me.

'Maître Chaumont,' he would say politely but firmly.

'Sorry, I think there's some mistake. My name is Smith, Mister Smith . . .' I would reply in my best English, hiding behind dark glasses and a scarf.

'Game's up, Maître Chaumont. We know who you are. Off you go.'

A few hours later I'd be back with my hair dyed blond. No sooner would I approach the door than the bouncer would shake his head, closing his eyes. Never again would I step inside the auction house.

For several weeks, I had spent every waking hour on Durit BN-657. A key component in the development of Formula 1 engines, this one small part would – so its inventor said – be the making of future Schumachers, Häkkinens and Alonsos. Two teams were disputing ownership of Durit, each claiming it had come out of its own research lab, and once again Chaumont–Chevrier legal partners had been drafted in to help. Since there was a fair bit of money at stake, Chevrier had shelved a more run-of-the-mill logo infringement case to provide back-up on Durit.

One lunchtime as he was getting his head around the case, I took a break to do what I liked best: taking a stroll around the exhibition halls at Drouot. Our office was fifty metres from the auction house – a deciding factor in the choice of premises. After wolfing down a sandwich and a bottle of lemonade, I headed inside. I glanced around a sale of Asian art. The sole lot consisted of a single erotic print showing a woman on very intimate terms with a giant octopus. Not being much of a one for bestiality or cephalopods, I moved swiftly on.

The first floor was overflowing with porcelain and rosewood chests of drawers. A weaponry sale was also taking place, drawing interest both from curious laymen and specialists in gunpowder and flintlocks. I headed to the basement. The sales down there were never hyped up in the way those held on the first floor were, and I had heard of people who bought exclusively from those auctions, reselling their purchases upstairs a few months later and living off the profits.

I ambled into a room where a collection of stamps was being exhibited ahead of a sale. My gaze wandered over depictions of the multicoloured feathers of tropical birds, the Italian lakes and profiles of the saviours of various countries. Having no great love of stamps, I carried on to the next room, which was devoted to taxidermy. From the hummingbird to the zebra, virtually the entire animal kingdom was represented here. An anteater caught my eye, but I sensed that to take such a thing home might not be the path to domestic harmony. And yet even if I had bought the entire collection and filled every room in the house with stuffed animals, the consequences would still have been far less than what was to come.

With weary eyes, dragging my feet, I entered room eight. Wardrobes, dressers, console tables and mirrors were piled high. The assorted collection of items resembled a jumble sale or a furniture clear-out, and contained nothing of style or value. I had almost reached the back of the room and was casting my eye over a display of cheap trinkets and ugly paintings on the walls when I saw it.

Sixty centimetres by forty. An eighteenth-century pastel in its original frame, of a man wearing a powdered wig and blue coat. In the top right-hand corner, a coat of arms I couldn't make out. Yet it was not the coat of arms that grabbed me, but the face. Transfixed, I could not tear my eyes away from it: the face was my own.

That portrait of me, painted two and a half centuries ago, which I came across in my forty-sixth year, was to turn out to be the high point of a collection I had been adding to for years. Each successive year, each successive object, and each successive docket had been leading me here to this late morning in room eight of Drouot Auction House. But it is to the very beginning of my life as a collector that we must return, to my very first purchase. I was nine years old and, being the good lawyer I am, I shall name that episode the 'Eraser Affair'.

Arthur, our faithful old basset hound, had died in his sleep from a massive heart attack. Two weeks later my mother bought an identical dog, but smaller. I found this attempt at replication tasteless and an insult to the memory of the first dog. I had suggested getting a black Dobermann, as a change from the basset hound, and had gone as far as to suggest a name, 'Sorbonne', in homage to Jean Rochefort's dog in *Angélique, Marquise des Anges*, which I had watched avidly in the Easter holidays. But my suggestion found no favour and my parents indulged their chronic lack of imagination and called the new dog Arthur as well.

Not long after, my mother dragged me with her on one of her afternoon shopping trips. Her favourite haunt was Old England on Boulevard des Capucines, an old-fashioned luxury department store where she insisted on buying me grey flannel trousers and navy-blue blazers. Ever since then I have had a horror of mouse grey and dark blue. I would not now wear a jacket in that shade of blue for anything, and I would rather go to work in my boxer shorts than in grey trousers. At that time, all I wanted was jeans, but denim was forbidden at the Cours Hattemer, the private school I attended. When she had tortured me by forcing me into hideous, outdated garments, my mother pressed on to the other department stores. There she tried on various outfits which, as usual, did not suit her. Then we went down to the stationery department; it was the beginning of the school year and I needed supplies for my pencil case. My mother bought me a yellow, banana-scented eraser, with the face of a panting Dobermann printed on it. No doubt followers of Freud would detect a hidden meaning behind this act: my mother was buying me an eraser in the image of the dog I had wanted so that I would forget all about my unfulfilled desire. I, on the other hand, only saw a lovely-looking scented eraser. A beautiful object that I had no intention of using – I would keep it. The next day after school I went off to look for another eraser with a dog's face on it. I found a green one decorated with a husky's head, in a little tobacconist's in the same road as the school. This one was apple-scented.

That evening I wrote in my diary: 'It's a collection when you have two and are looking for a third.'

That phrase was to become my motto.

'Uncle Edgar's so embarrassing,' my mother used to say of her father's brother with a sigh. Then my father would add a few intentionally incomprehensible words from which I could only make out 'crazy Aunty Edgar'. It was not until many years later that I understood how kind Uncle Edgar, whom, to my regret, I saw only once or twice a year, had come to have his mental health described in this way, and in the feminine.

'You're far more intelligent than your parents, little one,' Uncle Edgar once whispered to me.

I had stayed in the living room with him while my mother went to fetch some pre-dinner snacks. I remember staring into his watery blue eyes; he was in his mid-seventies by then. I found myself noticing his perfectly smooth cheek and the strange sheen that covered his whole face; my father's complexion was nothing like it. I raised my little hand to my uncle's elderly face and touched his cheek. A fine flesh-coloured powder came away on my fingertips, slightly shimmery, like the powder the maid, Céline, applied in front of the kitchen mirror.

My mother must have worn foundation too, but I never saw her put it on. She would shut herself in the bathroom to perform the ritual, despite the fact that little boys, and the men they become (while remaining little boys inside), find the sight of a woman applying her make-up fascinating. Only Céline let me watch her powdering her nose and shading her eyelids.

My eyes met my uncle's and I saw that, just like Céline, he had drawn a fine blue line underneath them, bringing out the colour of the iris. He watched me with tenderness as a sad, knowing smile appeared on his face.

'You'll understand when you grow up,' he murmured.

My mother returned with a plate of little biscuits and I closed my fist, rubbing my fingers against my palm as discreetly as possible to hide the secret of the uncle who made himself up like a girl.

Uncle Edgar brought all kinds of extraordinary things out of his pockets, describing each object in turn in the most wonderful way. I was reminded of that soft, rather camp voice of his years later when I stumbled on a French black-and-white film on cable TV. One of the supporting actors, Jean Tissier, had the exact same look, voice and mannerisms as my uncle.

As my parents watched with mild concern, Edgar would hand me things and ask me to study them 'intelligently and logically, my boy'. Cigarette cases, vanity sets, folding mirrors, fans, powder compacts, chocolate boxes and snuffboxes would always reveal some unexpected secret: a hidden mechanism, a dual purpose, or some other disguised use that amazed a little boy like me. Many times I asked my parents if I could visit Uncle Edgar's house to see his collections; the answer was always categorically no.

Edgar 'the crazy aunty' had scraped a living from writing about ballet and was famous for having penned an ode 'to the lithe tendons of pretty boys on points'. Edgar 'the collector' had been combing flea markets and auction houses for more than fifty years. He came from the poor side of the family and spent all his money on bric-a-brac and gigolos. And as he aged, his funds had dwindled.

The last time I saw Uncle Edgar, he spent a long time looking through my eraser collection, which now numbered ninety-five pieces of several different varieties including ones decorated with cars, characters and plants. My favourite carried a picture of a giant bean and a smell which was difficult to define, but which I decided to call sweet fennel. With his trademark black cape draped over his shoulders, he stared solemnly down at me from his six-foot-plus height.

'If we're to make a true collector of you, there's one thing you must understand: objects, *real* objects,' he said, wagging his finger for emphasis, 'carry the memory of their past owners.'

I looked up at him in turn, hanging back slightly, awed by the serious tone of the pronouncement.

'Do you understand?' he went on.

I nodded.

'What have you understood?' Uncle Edgar asked, smiling and kneeling down to my level.

'If they're old ...' I whispered.

'Go on, my boy ... If they're old ...'

'They keep people's souls,' I said all at once, holding my uncle's blue-eyed gaze.

He stopped smiling and appraised me with the utmost respect. Then he shook his head ever so slightly, which I took as a sign of approval – recognition, even.

The following day, I sold my entire eraser collection for the exorbitant sum of five hundred francs in cash. One break time, Marie-Amélie Clermont – eight years of age and an aspiring eraser collector – had stopped to admire the treasures I had brought to school in my satchel. She expressed an interest in acquiring the collection, but I refused. However, now that I had come to the conclusion that erasers didn't have a soul, since they didn't have a past, having never been owned by anyone but me, I had changed my mind and decided to part with them. The transaction took place at lunchtime. Marie-Amélie had gone home and pretended that Abbé Picard was collecting money on behalf of the poor children of Uganda. She persuaded her parents to give her five hundred francs, my asking price. That day – the day I doubled my money – was the day I learnt business sense; I was barely nine years old. On the first floor of the school at two o'clock, before the start of afternoon lessons, the collection changed hands. Marie-Amélie was now the proud owner of 109 erasers, including the 14 she already had. I held the legendary Pascal banknote tight in my clammy hand, and then slipped it into the back pocket of my grey flannel trousers.

Many years later I bumped into Marie-Amélie in the corridor of a courthouse, where she was awaiting the verdict of a dispute over her family estate on the island of Noirmoutier. I reminded her of the Eraser Affair.

She had no memory of it.

During my university years, I spent part of my student budget antique-hunting. I collected quite a few pieces and some I sold on, because sometimes objects lose their power: it breaks down over the years. When you point the Geiger counter of affection at certain pieces, it doesn't even react. It still crackles strongly for this eighteenth-century dolphin candlestick, but barely emits a hiss for that gold spoon with the French coat of arms, even though it had been coveted in the antique-shop window for many months. It becomes possible to sell the spoon with no regrets whilst the sale of the candlestick would be a wrench. This spontaneous emotional re-evaluation of objects has always been a mystery to me.

I had an aptitude for art dealing, doubling, trebling or even occasionally making back five times my initial outlay, and so I was able to avoid the odd jobs some of my friends had to take on. On occasion I could earn more in one afternoon than they earned in a month, a fact I was careful to keep to myself. But if I was successfully accumulating objects, I did not enjoy the same success with girls.

I didn't have a girlfriend at university, and regularly fell in love with girls who did not return my affections. Courting a girl who politely turns you down is as frustrating as gazing at an object in a museum case: you can look at it but it will never be yours.

Of course you could always shatter the glass, grab the object and run for the exit, but that's as unimaginable as flinging yourself roughly on a girl who has accepted an invitation for a drink and is explaining to you gently that she really likes you but …

I did not want to remain a virgin for much longer and once again I turned to my collector's instinct for a solution. I was used to obtaining what I wanted with money so I began to frequent prostitutes.

Following in the footsteps of my Uncle Edgar, who reinvested the proceeds from the sale of his works of art in the purchase of an hour with a male prostitute, I squandered my money in the arms of girls. There was Magali, Maya, Sophia, Marilyn, Samantha and many others besides. I was caught in an infernal spiral of expensive lust, which gradually consumed all my collections. That was how I came to sell my collection of snuffboxes made by convicts to, ironically enough, a policeman in the vice squad. The prisoners had let their erotic or murderous imaginations run wild as they carved fine designs into vegetable ivory. Next to go were my Baccarat crystal paperweights, with their replica flowers captured inside the glass. Then I let go of my leg-shaped ivory button-hooks, and finally my radiator caps with animal motifs. I traded objects for women.

A few years later, student parties would, of course, sometimes end in a conquest which led to an affair of sorts. But either the girls would leave me because I didn't want to commit to them, or I would leave them because I wasn't really interested. It's very difficult to speak words of love that you don't really feel; it's as if you are lying to yourself, which is even worse than lying to other people.

'You collect little dead things,' one of these girls had said to me.

She was a psychology student and probably saw me as an interesting case-study, even though she could not work me out. I also think she was annoyed with me for being more interested in my little dead things than in her. And that feeling of reproach would accompany me throughout my years as a collector.

When I was doing my PhD I met Jean Chevrier. He introduced me to Charlotte, a girl he had met recently on his MA course. A girl your friend is interested in is automatically more attractive.

In the early days of our relationship, Charlotte found my passion for antiques amusing, but later she found it irritating. As the years went by, two, then three, or even four or five paintings appeared on every wall of our apartment. Round paperweights sprouted on the dresser like mushrooms, bronze animals formed a veritable zoo and my empty snuffboxes could have held enough snuff for Napoleon's entire army.

Latterly, Charlotte had exiled my collections. An isolated emperor, my dictatorship extended across a territory of just fifteen square metres, and I spent long hours reviewing my static troops: millefiore glass paperweights, ironware, boxes, antique locks and autograph letters. My predecessors, Gulbenkian, Sacha Guitry and even Serge Gainsbourg, had had whole houses devoted to their innumerable collections; but I, at my lowly level, made do with a 'study'. I dreamt of having somewhere like Sacha's wonderful house at 18 Avenue Élisée Reclus filled with his fabulous collections, now dispersed. I did possess one relic of his, an anonymous sketch of Napoleon on Elba, stamped on the back 'from Sacha Guitry's collection'. The Emperor was gazing out to sea, lost in contemplation. He still saw a great future for himself. Like him, I was also going to make my escape.

But for much longer than a hundred days.

'Number forty-six... Restoration mercury-gilt mirror ...' called the auctioneer.

'Very handsome piece with angel motif,' added the expert alongside him, speaking into the crackling microphone in a dreary monotone.

Standing in my usual spot at the back of the room, I waited for number forty-eight with pounding heart. Once again I felt the rush that always comes at auctions: the fast pace, the queasy combination of excitement and nerves. It was like driving at top speed with a blindfold on. Would I get what I had set my heart on, my prized portrait? Did I have the funds to fuel the race?

I had hurried back to the office and cancelled all my afternoon meetings, giving no explanation. I was certainly not prepared to leave a written bid and risk seeing the picture go to another buyer.

The portrait and I had been locked in a long, wordless showdown, as I stood facing it, my reflection almost imprinting itself on the protective glass, before I went into the office to enquire about the price. I looked expectantly at the young intern behind the desk, waiting for her to notice the uncanny resemblance. While she scrolled down the photocopied price list, I tried to attract her attention.

'This portrait ... is astonishing! And so lifelike!' I raved.

She was too preoccupied to notice any likeness.

'Number forty-eight has an estimate of between fifteen hundred and two thousand euros, Monsieur.'

Not cheap, but I could afford it. And I absolutely had to have it.

'Do you really not know who the sitter is? There's a coat of arms after all ...' I went on, still apparently staring at the girl a little too intently, as she immediately looked away.

'No, our expert hasn't researched it.'

'What a shame. I'll have to do it myself.'

'Would you like to leave a bid?'

'Certainly not. I'm coming to the auction,' I said, still not averting my gaze.

'Anything else, Monsieur?'

'No.'

I left, making way for an old man with a hearing aid. The girl had to raise her voice to tell him about the porcelain. I returned to my portrait and stood directly beneath it, propping my arm up against the red velvet ledge that ran along the wall and trying to catch the eye of other visitors. Without success.

*

'Seven hundred!'

The mercury-gilt mirror had just gone under the hammer.

'Number forty-seven, a pair of girandoles. Would you show them, please?'

The assistant clumsily waved the candlesticks around like bunches of leeks.

'Five hundred! No takers at five hundred? That's a steal for girandoles! Four hundred, then! Fifty, now you're waking up, five hundred, we're getting there, fifty, six hundred …'

'Monsieur Steiner?' the auctioneer turned to a dealer, who shook his head.

'Six hundred on my right,' the bid caller went on. 'The gentleman with blond hair,' he added under his breath.

The hammer struck. The bid caller headed towards a blond gentleman holding a slip of paper in his hand.

'Number forty-eight, portrait.'

My turn had come. The pastel was being carried in by the assistant.

'Now that's lovely!' the auctioneer exclaimed at once.

Hearing him talk it up like this made me suddenly worried.

'And we haven't tried to identify the painter or sitter?'

The anonymity business seemed to niggle him too.

'No, we have not. We haven't had time,' the expert replied curtly, visibly put out by the auctioneer's remark.

The girl who had helped me earlier was discreetly

chewing gum and looking over at me. She glanced down at a notebook, picked up the phone and dialled a number.

I had decided my strategy would be to hold back in the early stages before jumping in around the fifteen hundred mark, taking the other bidders by surprise.

'Let's start at one thousand. One thousand euros! One two, one four, one five …'

I locked eyes with the auctioneer and my hand shot up.

'Eight,' he said when he saw me.

'Two thousand,' the bid caller shot back.

'Two two,' the auctioneer continued at my nod.

'Two four,' he added immediately, turning to his left.

'Two six, eight.'

'Three thousand, written bid,' the expert announced.

'Three two,' the caller went on, having just clocked a new bidder.

'Three four,' the auctioneer called out as I raised my hand.

'Three thousand four hundred!'

'Three six, three eight.'

'Four thousand by written bid,' the expert carried on.

'Four five,' the girl on the phone suddenly threw in.

I glared at her as if the poor woman was responsible for the instructions she had been given. The auctioneer turned and tilted his chin in my direction.

'Seven,' he said at my nod.

'Five thousand,' the girl replied.

I nodded again.

'Five two,' the auctioneer continued.

There was a pause while the girl talked into the phone.

'Five thousand two hundred euros!' the auctioneer cried.

'Six thousand,' the girl came back.

'Do you want to go to six five?' the auctioneer asked me.

I agreed.

'Six thousand five hundred euros!'

'Seven thousand,' the girl replied.

How high could I go? I was beginning to feel uneasy.

'Five!' I said aloud.

'Eight thousand,' the girl responded.

'Two!' I shouted, trying to slow things down.

'Five!' she added.

'Seven!' I responded.

'Nine thousand?' the auctioneer asked her.

She agreed.

'Nine five,' I shot back.

My inhibitions had floated away and there was a strange feeling of lightness about me. Nothing else mattered now; I was acting as if this day might be my last.

'Nine thousand five hundred,' the auctioneer repeated.

'Six,' the girl replied.

'Eight,' the auctioneer came back when I blinked my assent.

The girl repeated my bid down the line, I saw her lips moving, and then she looked up at the auctioneer and shook her head.

'Nine thousand eight hundred going once!' the bid caller repeated as the girl put down the phone.

'Nine thousand eight hundred going twice!' the auctioneer announced to the room, loud and clear.

Strike the bloody hammer, you bastard, I said to myself.

He held it in mid-air. I was dripping with sweat and having difficulty breathing. Nine thousand eight hundred euros. There was no way I could go any higher. With the fees on top, I was already looking at a bill of nearly twelve thousand euros. If a new bid was placed, I could not raise it. I wanted to throw myself at him, bend his arm to the table and force him to bring down the wretched hammer.

'All done at nine thousand eight hundred euros?' he asked, drawing out every word.

At last, I saw the gavel begin to move. There it went, whooshing down towards the table. Any second, it would strike. Now … now … Yes! The portrait was mine.

The glory of pastel. The powder was finely applied to the paper in several translucent layers, harmoniously superimposed on each other. It reminded me of the powder that had stayed on my fingers the day I touched Uncle Edgar's cheek.

'Fascinating,' I murmured, studying the face as I swallowed a mouthful of Bowmore.

I had needed the whisky to calm myself down. Since I had taken the afternoon off, I had gone straight home and placed my portrait on the sofa in the living room. The pastel rendered the shimmering blue silk of the suit admirably. The powdered Louis XV wig ended in fine curls at my ears. Of course, at the back I would have had an elegant cadogan ponytail tied with a ribbon of the same blue, as was the fashion in the eighteenth century.

The eyes stared back at me, their colour indefinable, but given an eternal sparkle by the little dot of white chalk the artist had used on each of the pupils. I walked to the left then to the right of the portrait. The eyes followed me. I had read that only the Mona Lisa could do that. Which was obviously false since this portrait of me could do the same.

At first sight the background of the portrait appeared to be dark brown, but in reality my character was set against a backdrop of various colours. Brown, green, terracotta, slate, the background was made up of infinite shades of powder. At the top on the right, the artist had reproduced the coat of arms that would allow the man in the wig to be identified.

I downed the rest of my drink. Charlotte would be home soon; I wouldn't admit the price I had paid for the picture. That was out of the question. A small adjustment to our bank account would suffice to hide the €11,760. Since the sale of my collection of erasers, I had retained a liking for cash transactions. So I had a little safe in my study containing a lovely bundle of five-hundred euro notes. This money had been earned from some 'friendly' consultations for clients who were not actually clients. My work had its shady side, sleeping in the safe in my study. I often reflected that the bundle was not there in that room by chance. It was an integral part of my collections. I collected purple five hundreds. Now they would all have to go. But no matter.

Fifteen hundred. Eighteen hundred euros. Yes, that was a price I could admit to Charlotte; she would accept that. If I told her it had cost €11,760, she was bound to fly into a rage. Leaving aside the financial aspect, I couldn't wait to see her reaction to the portrait. I poured myself a second whisky. This time I added some ice and went back into the living room to kneel in front of the pastel, as if worshipping myself. My nose ... it was my nose. And my mouth as well – the artist had picked out the shape with a little red powder to distinguish it from the hue of the cheeks ... And those ears were also exactly the same as mine. The sound of the key in the lock made me turn around.

'Are you there?'

'I'm in here,' I replied, emptying my whisky glass so that Charlotte would not know how much I had poured myself.

'You're home early,' she said, taking off the delicate purple silk scarf she always wore in early summer.

She caught sight of the portrait. 'You've been back to Drouot? You have to stop doing that, Pierre-François, you're encroaching on the living room again.'

She came forward and I watched her, waiting for her reaction. 'Do you notice anything?'

'What am I supposed to notice?' she snapped in irritation.

'What are you supposed to notice? The resemblance to me! It's unbelievable how much he looks like me. It is me!'

'What are you talking about?' she said, with disgust. 'He looks nothing like you; whatever do you mean? But in any case I don't want to see it in the living room. You'll have to put it in your study.'

Stunned and stupefied, I watched Charlotte leave the room. In a state of semi-consciousness that had nothing to do with alcohol, I heard her footsteps in the corridor leading to the kitchen, the fridge door opening and then more footsteps. She returned with a glass of orange juice which she drank defiantly as we looked at each other in silence.

Nothing would ever be the same between us again.

That must have been the night my dreams started. Or my dream, rather. For a while I even considered seeing a shrink about it, though I already had a sense of what it might mean. It recurred throughout the time of my research, forcing its way into my head every two or three nights.

During my sleep, while my body was safely stretched out under the covers, my mind wandered to unfamiliar places. Before this point, I had only had dreams of the erotic variety, and even then, rarely. A few years earlier, one such dream had caused me to develop an accidental obsession with our young local florist. For several weeks she kept coming to me in my sleep, begging me to do the most unspeakable things to her in her shop – invariably on the shelf with the cactuses and carnivorous plants. I ended up having to change florist. It had become impossible to go in and buy Charlotte a bunch of roses without pornographic images from the previous night flashing before my eyes. I started frequenting another florist much further up the boulevard. The large, moustachioed man who tied my bouquets there never featured in any dreams.

There was nothing sexy about the dream that now haunted my sleep. I was walking through a devastated landscape and the pavement, or perhaps the earth itself, beneath my feet had been replaced with ash. The fronts of the buildings were also coated in ash. There was no way of knowing if this was now or some point in the past. The only time I could remember seeing such an apocalyptic scene of a lifeless city covered in dust was after September 11. But in my dream no catastrophe had taken place. The ghost town I was walking through had long been shrouded in ash and silence; perhaps it had always been that way. I kept going along the empty streets, my suit covered in dust, as I searched for signs of life. There were none. Emerging into a small square like a Venetian *campo*, I came upon a guillotine, far more modern than the contraptions used during the Revolution. I couldn't help thinking it must have been made quite recently, but what was it for? 'We got rid of the death penalty,' I told myself. 'So who's been making this?' I was mulling this over while inspecting the guillotine from every angle when suddenly invisible hands grabbed me from behind and began to lift me off the ground.

I was being dragged towards the scaffold, almost flat on my belly. 'I beg your pardon? I beg your pardon?' I kept saying, which I recalled was a frequent expression of my uncle's, one that I never used. I felt as light as a feather and, far from putting up a fight and screaming, I was thinking how it would not be uninteresting to feel the 'chill' on my neck that the device's inventor spoke of, just to experience it, out of pure curiosity, since afterwards I would merely have to take my head from the basket and put it back on my neck for everything to return to normal.

The guillotine fell in cocoon-like silence and I barely felt the supposed chill; this was slightly disappointing. I peered into the basket which ought to have caught my head, but there was no sign of it. I'm not sure how I realised this, as I was supposed no longer to have a head, but dreams have a way of getting around such minor details.

This mystery of the missing head filled me with concern. I knew I had to find it before I could go back to work, as I wouldn't be let back into the office if no one could recognise me.

I was gripped by anxiety, and then panic. I had to get my head back and there was no one I could turn to for help. I was getting so worked up I thought I was about to have a heart attack, when suddenly the whole scene lit up.

The ash was replaced by fine, hot, honey-coloured sand. I was no longer wearing my loafers and could feel the sand burning the soles of my feet. I noticed that my shirt and tie had gone and I had nothing on but my black suit trousers. The guillotine had disappeared too. A stunningly beautiful woman was standing in front of me. I knew she was beautiful, but I couldn't see her. I moved towards her and realised she was holding my head in her hands. She was also coming towards me, and distressingly

I could not make out her facial features. At last she placed my head on my shoulders. All at once I came back to life and no sooner had I opened my mouth and eyes than her lips met mine in a kiss.

I still couldn't see her face, but this no longer bothered me as it had done moments before. I didn't care what she looked like; I was in love. Madly in love.

At that moment, a thought occurred to me: why had she been holding my head? I started to pull away in order to ask her.

The question was never answered because at that moment I always woke up, bringing both dream and kiss to a close.

I woke feeling bereft. I wanted nothing more than to find that woman again, even if it meant going back to the dusty city and the guillotine. I tried to go straight back to sleep, but I could never return to the dream.

The evening the portrait arrived we were having a couple of friends round for dinner. Over the aperitif I could not resist showing off my latest find. I slipped off to my study and returned proudly carrying the portrait. I placed it on an armchair and waited for a reaction. Charlotte was going to be embarrassed when her lack of visual sense was publicly exposed. But what I so ardently desired did not in the event come about, and it amused Charlotte to highlight my disappointment by declaring: 'Pierre-François thinks the picture looks like him!'

Our friends responded with incredulous exclamations.

Was it possible that no one but me could see the resemblance? Yes, it was possible. Simon's days were spent staring at screens monitoring the Bourse and Nathalie's counting her stock of Chanel suits over and over. It was hardly surprising that people like that were incapable of noticing.

Their ways of seeing had been ruined by modern life, their brains dulled by gazing at magazine covers and advertising billboards. They could no longer perceive anything.

Just before going to bed I reached for my bedside book, *Monsieur de Phocas* by Jean Lorrain, searching for a sentence on looking. I feverishly consulted the entire book. There were many sentences on looking, since Monsieur de Phocas had a veritable fixation with eyes, claiming to be able to detect all sorts of mortiferous and erotic crimes by studying irises. But I remembered a short paragraph on modern eyes and their inability to see.

'Modern eyes? They have no soul; they no longer look up to heaven. Even the most pure are only concerned with the immediate. Vulgar lust, petty self-interest, greed, vanity, prejudice, cowardly appetites and envy. Those are the abominable emotions swarming in today's eyes. We have the souls of notaries and cooks. That's why the eyes of the portraits in museums are so spectacular; they reflect prayers and tortures, regrets and remorse. Eyes are the source of tears; the source has run dry, the eyes are dulled; only faith makes them come alive, but you can't reignite cinders. We walk with our eyes fixed on our shoes: our expressions are the colour of mud. When eyes appear beautiful to us, it is because they are full of the splendour of lies, because they hark back to a portrait, to a gaze in a museum or because they regret the past.'

Standing in the middle of the bedroom, I finished reading aloud. I had read with such vehemence that I felt out of breath. Lying on the bed, Charlotte was watching me in silence. She was holding a women's magazine. On the cover a young blonde woman in a blue bikini was smiling vacuously.

'What are you implying?' she asked calmly.

'You don't know how to look,' I replied. 'You no longer know how to see; Jean Lorrain was already writing that a hundred years ago.'

'I can't see that you look like the man in the portrait, is that what you mean? Well, have it your way,' she said, turning back to her magazine.

I could see the cover headline: 'Me and my breasts'

Jean Lorrain's prose held no interest for my wife. I felt as if I had been slapped and I was about to ask her if that was all she and her breasts had to say about my portrait, when Charlotte looked up at me. 'How much did you pay for your picture?'

'It was €11,760 including costs.'

I have only a hazy memory of the domestic scene that followed. When I think of it, what comes to mind is the ceiling of my living room.

Charlotte rose swiftly from the bed to go into the living room, as if it was essential that the portrait should also witness the scene. She raised her eyes skywards then began to scream. I thought then that it was the perfect illustration of that expression 'to raise your eyes skywards'. A few years earlier I had had the ceiling redone by an artist from the national museums. In the sky he had painted there were little cumulus clouds tinted pink on the edge of the mouldings. It was glorious. All the five-hundred euro notes in the secret safe had been spent on it. That evening, I wished the atmospheric pressure on my ceiling would change, to make the cotton-wool clouds turn into huge dark blocks, followed by thunder and a lightning bolt that would strike the woman shrieking in front of me.

It was not the cost of the painting that mattered, nor Charlotte's reproaches and yelpings over my recklessness at the auction. What mattered was that she had not seen what had immediately struck me, the resemblance between myself and the portrait. Charlotte could not see me. That was the only possible explanation. For how long had I been invisible to her and to others?

Then Charlotte snatched the book out of my hands. She turned it over and read out the author's biography in a triumphant tone.

'"Jean Lorrain, gay dandy, make-up wearer, ether addict; he is the chronicler of decadence"; so that's the kind of books you read!' she said before going on to mention a passion for objects, financial ruin and the habits of Uncle Edgar which I had imprudently mentioned to her.

The distant coldness that existed between us over the next few days reached its height at bedtime. I no longer desired her in any way at all. I now considered her nothing but a rival, a soul who had always refused to be in tune with mine. An enemy, in fact. As if she were aware of how I now viewed her, Charlotte rallied her troops, drawn from amongst our close friends.

'Show them your portrait!' she would cry in the living room over the aperitifs, or over dinner.

Always followed by, 'Pierre-François thinks the painting looks like him …'

One morning, I took my portrait to my office. After half an hour spent looking for a hammer, a nail and a pair of pliers, I yanked out the hook that for ten years had held the old canvas-mounted advert for the French Line. I was just hanging my portrait up, whilst balancing on a shaky stool, when Chevrier pushed my door open. Sweating and red in the face, I turned towards him.

'Who's that?' he asked innocently.

I decided to put the French Line back in its place and return the pastel to the apartment.

A few days later I got up in the middle of the night to try something that had occurred to me as I was about to fall asleep. What if the pastel only spoke to me? Perhaps it contained secret vibrations that acted like a screen reflecting the gaze of the person looking at it.

I laid the painting flat on the parquet floor of the study. On all fours in my pyjamas, I began to try to make a pendulum turn above the painting. Would it turn clockwise or anti-clockwise? I could not remember the basics of how pendulums worked. I looked up. Charlotte was staring at me in silence from the door.

'Try using a table,' she said evenly, before going back to bed.

Perhaps turning to the occult was not such a ridiculous idea. I began to search through a large tome I had bought at university: a late-nineteenth-century edition, which nevertheless reproduced very precisely the recipes and magical preparations used by the witches and wizards of our regions. The chapter devoted to potions for 'clairvoyance' particularly caught my eye. It set out all the mixtures that could be concocted to open someone's eyes to whatever it was their brain refused to accept. It was exactly what I needed.

'The blood of a bat, an apple picked by a young virgin, powder of rat's claw, the feather of an owl. Crush the ingredients and leave them to macerate in mead for seven days and seven nights before serving.'

As I would be unlikely to find these little-used products in my local Monoprix, and it would also be awkward to ask my greengrocer about his sex life, I fell back on butterfly lemonade with unicorn powder, a little easier to make. A unicorn's horn was just, in fact, a narwhal's tusk, and I had one in my study. The thirteen butterflies mentioned could easily be obtained from my collection. It seemed to me that it would be quite easy to prepare the concoction and I was proposing to trick Charlotte and the next visitors to the apartment into drinking it, when I noticed a little stipulation: the butterflies had to be alive before going into the pot. City fauna being extremely limited, hunting down thirteen butterflies, even over several years, would be all but impossible.

In the end I gave up on these gastronomic experiments and the possibility of convincing my circle.

'Go and get your picture, Pierre-François.'

'No.'

'Why not?'

'My collections are my affair and I'm not sharing them,' I replied tartly that evening, gulping down my orange juice.

Our guests and my wife watched me in silence until one of them ventured timidly, 'And how is work? What case are you on at the moment?'

I embarked on an account of Durit BN-657 which held absolutely no interest for me. Now all my attention was focused on coats of arms. I spent my evenings on the internet poring over the hundreds of pages devoted to heraldry. I was investigating myself and I went at it with all the determination of a solitary navigator in the midst of a storm.

The coat of arms which graces my amazing portrait had turned into a full-blown obsession. It was the key to unmasking the figure in the picture, almost a sample of the man's DNA. On the left side of the shield, a black cat stood on its hind legs facing a medieval sword that was pointing upwards; on the right was a kind of carrot in human form. The cat and the sword were on a white background, the vegetable on black. The longer I looked at it, the more the cat seemed to be performing a magic trick; the two clawed paws it was holding out seemed to be exerting some untold power over the sword, lifting it off the ground by willpower alone. That evening, while comparing the coat of arms to a roughly similar design found among the 457 pages of results for 'family crests of France' online, I heard Charlotte's voice from the dining room. Over the past few days, I had noticed a slight shrillness creeping into my darling wife's voice.

Admittedly I had taken to spending entire evenings lying on the sofa flicking through page after page of dictionaries and documents discovered on the internet.

When Charlotte entered the room, I didn't look up from my reading. All I saw were her legs: disapproval in every step, exasperation in the ankles.

'Din-ner is rea-dy!' she shouted for the third time.

From the next room, I thought I heard the crystal chandelier – picked up at a flea market one summer afternoon five years earlier – tinkle slightly, probably on account of my wife's voice. I pushed my wireless mouse away scornfully and followed her into the dining room, as apparently nothing mattered more at that moment than eating avocado vinaigrette.

'How's your research coming along?' she asked, all sweetness and light.

'Badly. I've hit a wall,' I grumbled.

'We'll never know who it is,' she said, taking a bite of avocado.

'We will, I swear we will!' I replied a little over-dramatically, which made Charlotte giggle.

As her high-pitched laughter rose towards the ceiling, I gave the chandelier a glance.

Like the oil in my avocado, which sat on the surface of the heavy vinaigrette, it was all stubbornly refusing to come together. This was what I was so desperately searching for, for everything to blend and produce some kind of alchemy that would alter matter, even life itself. For the past three weeks, I had been calling upon every neuron I possessed, a good hundred billion of them, to try to put a name to this mysterious coat of arms.

'Eat your avocado.'

I made the mistake of sighing and pulling a face. Like a mongoose, Charlotte immediately seized upon my expression and the few decilitres of air that had just been expelled from my lungs.

'You don't like it? Is that it?' she challenged me.

'Yes, I do, it's very nice ...' I said, scrambling to save myself. 'It's lovely, and the presentation, the way you've arranged the slices of lemon and pepper, is really ... exquisite.'

'Exquisite,' she muttered poisonously, as if I had just insulted her.

She put down her fork and looked me straight in the eye. The anger she had been trying so hard to contain suddenly burst out.

'I'm not hungry and I've had enough!' she shouted. 'You can eat by yourself, Pierre-François Chaumont!'

This time there was no need to check my crystal chandelier to appreciate just how far the pitch had risen. I was about to trot out a few soothing words, the way men do ('Oh come on, darling'), but it was too late. The bedroom door was already being slammed shut, opening again seconds later with a shout of 'You get the quail out!'

The door banged shut once more and the apartment was quiet again, with just a slight hum coming from the computer hard drive.

A few moments later, I took four perfectly cooked quail out of the oven. The birds still had their heads intact. As they lay in profile in the earthenware dish, I began to examine them, intrigued. Four quail lying side by side, not quite perfectly aligned, beaks turned westward. Was there a coat of arms depicting four quail?

It must have been the quail or possibly the delicious burgundy. I wanted to make love in spite of our quarrel at dinner. In fact, was that not the best way for a couple to make up? An argument could produce some excited anticipation, and so I approached the bed quietly in the dark. I wanted to make love to her but most of all I wanted to rediscover the young girl I had fallen for at university.

Where had that Charlotte gone? The girl with long hair who used to wear a headscarf tied round her head in summer. The girl who organised cheap holidays for our little group of university friends to far-flung places: Afghanistan, Jordan, Yemen, the Sahara. That time was long past; everyone had married, everyone had children. The time for friendships and for taking off on trips had gone for ever. Charlotte had cut her hair. She was no longer the free, enthusiastic woman I had married; and yet that was the person I wanted to find again for a moment.

'What are you doing?'

'I'm caressing you,' I said softly, 'I'm caressing these breasts ... which belong to me,' I added hopefully and somewhat lecherously.

'Leave me alone,' she replied, turning away.

'And what if I don't want to leave you alone,' I persevered, still speaking softly.

'Stop it ... I hope at least that you ate the quail?'

I sat up in the bed and studied Charlotte, my eyes having grown accustomed to the gloom. I looked at her neck and her back. She was a huge cold fish wallowing in my sheets, totally hostile, an icy, frigid mermaid. What had come over me to want to make love with her? If I were honest with myself, I hadn't desired her in the least for the past month. Yet I had loved her. I had adored her body, her legs, her breasts and that blush that spread up her neck as she came. Could you suddenly stop loving someone because of a misunderstanding?

But then, had everything we had lived through together just been a misunderstanding? Like an antique that you buy, love and cherish, and which for years makes you think of all the troubled times it has passed through – the Hundred Years War, the French Revolution, the Siege of Moscow – but which you notice one morning is nothing but a vulgar fake made ten years ago.

Had I made a mistake with my life? What was I doing as a lawyer? If I really thought about it, I spent most of my time defending the progress of modernity, through the patents I protected. But it was the past I loved. I was betraying my convictions. I was an impostor. I should have become an antiques dealer and made money from my fabulous collections, studied at the École du Louvre or the French Library school, become a museum curator, an art critic, an exhibitor at the Biennale des Antiquaires, initiating Californian millionaires into the sensual delights of Fragonard, they who were only familiar with Cadillac chrome.

And what about my wife; had I made a mistake there too? What was I doing with this partner who rejected me, who laughed at my interests and confined all my wonderful objects, which many an interior designer would have envied, to one little room in the apartment? Perhaps Charlotte would have liked to confine me to my study too? All she would have had to do was turn the key in the lock and she would have been free of me. Perhaps I was no more than a little dead thing to her? A thing that got in her way more than any object from my collections, a thing that talked, breathed and wanted to caress her breasts.

Feeling dizzy, I went and sat back down in front of my computer. What had I been doing all these years? Perhaps just filling a powder keg ready to explode at any moment. All that had been lacking was the spark that would ignite the conflagration of my life. And now it was here; for three weeks it had been under my nose every day. The source of my torment was the portrait, the one with the indecipherable coat of arms. Since it had been in the apartment, I had felt my existence dissolving as surely as a sugar cube in water.

I reached for my mouse. The black-and-white screensaver I had downloaded of Sacha Guitry's *salon* disappeared immediately, to be replaced by the website devoted to coats of arms. I clicked onto the next page.

In the centre appeared a sort of triangular shield with a cat, a sword and a carrot in human form. I moved the cursor to the coat of arms and clicked again. With that simple action I activated the only virus capable of destroying my existence, which had been so well protected up until that moment.

http://www.herald-defranc.org/index_f.tm/trad.html-
87k-france-bourgogne-dom/de/m@ndragore

Mandragore. The lineage of the Seigneurs of Mandragore
can be traced back to the twelfth century. Both the family
and the estate take their name from the fabled mandrake
plant, still occasionally found among the vines of the
Mandragore estate today. To find out more, click here:
Mandrake, plant.

Mandrake, plant: n. lat. *mandragora*. Plant which grows in
warm climates whose knobby forked root is said to resemble
the human form. The mandrake was once credited with
magical properties and was used in witchcraft.

So the human carrot on the family's shield symbolised the
sorcerer's plant. It had been a long time since I had heard
of the mythical mandrake, and I never imagined it would
be my gateway to the coat of arms.

'It's all coming together ...' I muttered to myself.

I had a vague feeling that everything was falling into

place that night, while Charlotte was tucked beneath the covers. And wasn't tonight a full moon, when according to legend the magical plant should be dug up? I stood up and lifted the net curtain at the living-room window. The moon may have been full, but it was refusing to show itself.

A history of the coat of arms of the Rivaille-Mandragore de Villardier family

Blazon: 'Impaled. At sinister, sable, a mandrake of gold; at dexter, argent, a cat passant proper, armed and langued gules, holding in its paws a long sword of gold. Motto "None but me". War-cry "innocent". Supporters two lions. A coronet.'

On his return from the fifth crusade, Aymeric de Rivaille, Comte de Villardier, Seigneur of Bourgogne, brought mandrake plants back from the far-off countries he had visited. Having been wounded in Palestine, he was treated using extracts of the plant, known for its anaesthetic properties. Though the plant was already considered maleficent, the holy Church allowed him to grow it on his land in order to continue his treatment. Suckers from mandrake plants are still sometimes found among the vines at Rivaille. Their shrivelled roots no longer reach the impressive size they once did. The Rivaille lands became known as Mandragore, meaning mandrake, and the family adopted this curious name for their own. This is what is represented on the 'sinister' side of the shield.

The symbolism of the cat, which occupies the 'dexter' side, is more difficult to interpret. The cat is as rare a heraldic charge as the mandrake; leopards, *lions léopardés* and lions rampant are far more common. Furthermore, the Rivaille cat is blazoned as 'armed and langued gules', terms normally employed for lions, meaning that the black (sable) cat has a red tongue and claws. There are a number of conflicting theories as to its origins. The interpretation given widest currency is as follows: Henri de Rivaille (1540–83) was riding across his lands when he was caught in a storm. Frightened by the din, the horse bolted, and Henri would have been doomed but for a cat sitting on a branch overhanging the path, which took fright at the sight of the steed galloping towards it. Its fur stood on end and it meowed so loudly that the horse stopped in its tracks. Henri saw the hand of God in the behaviour of the cat which, by halting his mount's uncontrollable charge, had saved his life. The cat was taken home by the count. Among the records of staff and residents of the chateau at the time, the name 'Innocent' appears often; it also features as the war-cry above the family shield. It is possible that Innocent was the name of the cat.

Afterwards, Henri de Rivaille issued an edict: it would henceforth be forbidden to chase, hunt or kill any cat on his lands. Each of these offences was punishable by death. He also had his coat of arms redesigned to feature the cat, the mandrake of his forebear, and the family sword. The only one of these charges to appear in the arms known as 'old Rivaille', the first coat of arms of the house of Rivaille, was the sword; the shield was 'azure, a sword in pale argent', which is to say, vertical. The attitude of the cat 'passant', standing on its hind legs, could be interpreted as follows: the cat saves the sword of the house of Rivaille, its power, glory and descendants, protecting the lands of Mandragore for all time.

Wine

Clos Mandragore, premier cru 'les esprits'.

Since Aimé-Charles de Rivaille took over from his father upon his death in 1998, he has invested heavily in remodelling the cellars and buying new equipment. The quality of the wines he produces on the finest land of the village of Chassagne-Montrachet has improved consistently over the years. This Chassagne red has an intense ruby colour. Its maturity is apparent on the nose, with aromas of ripe, dark fruits. Blackcurrant and raspberry, with subtle and well-blended woody notes. Full-bodied with an appealing and perfectly balanced mouthfeel (fruits, tannins and alcohol) that is sophisticated, elegant and fruity. A complex and well-rounded Chassagne wine.

The Chateau

Regular and symmetrical in appearance, the Chateau of Mandragore is typical of the French classical style: a main building with an elaborately decorated pediment adjoined by two perpendicular wings with tiled roofs and a large, round, slate-roofed tower at either end. Adjacent to the western tower is a stable bearing the arms of the house of Mandragore. The estate is surrounded by wide moats leading into two ornamental ponds and is approached through a courtyard, over a hectare in size, which was planted with a rose garden by Hubert-Félix de Rivaille in 1882. *Watch slideshow (12 photos)*.

When I opened my eyes again I immediately saw the black-and-white photo of Sacha Guitry's *salon*. The screen had gone into sleep mode. How long had I been asleep? My head was full of the images of the slideshow: a huge building with white walls and tiled roof that appeared to be suspended over the water, then a massive round tower bordered by green grass, a rose garden on the scale of a park, the multicoloured flowers bathed in sunshine. The walls inside the building were lined with red fabric and covered in paintings with gilded wooden frames. There were also crystal chandeliers, carpets, armchairs and Louis XV banquettes.

Twelve minutes past five was the time showing at the top of the screen. I felt a draught on my face – I had opened the window slightly for a breath of fresh air. The calm of the morning was only disturbed by a few snatches of song from birds I could not see. I had not known there were so many in the city and, in the morning light, the silence and the chirping of the invisible birds gave me a strange sensation of harmony. I decided to soak up the peaceful atmosphere by taking a stroll along the boulevard.

I wandered as far as the gates of Parc Monceau and followed the railings back towards the Courcelles crossroads. On the opposite pavement an old man was walking his basset hound. It was rather early for a walk. Perhaps the old man was an insomniac and his dog had become one too by osmosis. I was reminded of our old dog, Arthur, of his successor and of my collection of erasers. As I walked calmly, I began to have flashbacks of my past. I pictured the lecture theatres at my law school – they were deserted. Deserted and silent, too, was my office in Rue de la Grange-Batelière. I could make out the winking red light on the fax machine. As I walked, images came to me, neither really moving nor exactly fixed; little strips of Super-8, spliced together in a completely random order.

Curiously I could not see myself in any of the images. Not myself, nor Charlotte, nor my colleagues, nor the crowds in the sale rooms; not even anonymous passers-by who should have been in these photograms. There was no human presence, as if there had been a mass exodus or a nuclear war.

I went to a bistro on Boulevard de Courcelles and ordered coffee at an outside table. I was the only customer and the waiter setting out tables and chairs on the terrace paid no attention to me. Occasionally a car passed and I noticed that the sound of the tyres was different in the silence of the early morning. Something like a waterfall. Then nothing. Boulevard de Courcelles had also been deserted; there seemed to be barely more than five or six people in the whole arrondissement. The waiter, me, the woman behind the bar, the man in the car who was already on his way to Place des Ternes … And it was best like this. What remained were the essentials; the superfluous parts of life had been eliminated during the night as if by magic.

'End of the world – beginning of the world', these two propositions jostled in my head and I could not tell which was more appropriate this morning.

Without knowing it, I was already being erased.

I opened the door to our apartment quietly and closed it again carefully. I trod on the parquet of the living room, making sure that the boards did not creak. Why was I doing that? What could be more normal than opening one's own front door then going in and sitting down on one's sofa? It was the most reassuring of acts. Yet I was not reassured; I was now walking about my own home like a thief. I didn't want Charlotte to wake up, I didn't want to have to explain myself. I took the portrait from my study and laid it flat on the floor. In a cupboard I found a large roll of bubble wrap – courtesy of Drouot – and I wrapped the portrait before carefully taping the edges. A few minutes later down in the garage I leant the package against the back of the front seats of my Jaguar. I closed the back door then got into the driving seat. I wanted to know. I would go to the source. Once there I was sure I would get to the bottom of the mystery.

*

As I drove out of Paris the radio changed station and started playing the first notes of *Melody Nelson*. Bass chords popped like soap bubbles, then the voice of Serge Gainsbourg, pure, hypnotic and dirge-like, began to recite the strange poem: 'The wings of the Rolls Royce brushed past the pylons ...'

I was not driving a Rolls and there weren't any pylons I could see ... yet I did feel I was brushing past my existence one last time. At a hundred and eighty kilometres an hour, the few micrometres that separated the rubber of my tyres from the road were raising me above the warm path that had been my life. I was taking off.

The smoke from my Benson & Hedges Gold wafts upwards in the candlelight. In the heat, beads of sweat are beginning to form on my brow and it crosses my mind that I ought to put a minibar in the shed to provide ice for my whisky. If there's a heatwave, visits to my collections will become impossible, to say nothing of the fire risk. I stand up and walk towards a piece I still haven't found a satisfactory home for in my makeshift cabinet of curiosities, a rosewood liqueur caddy. In the centre of its fine marquetry, just above the keyhole, sits a small copper plate on which the words 'Lord Byron, Venezia' can be read.

My gaze falls on a heavy black cape hanging from a coat hanger and I swallow my last gulp of whisky with a smile.

'One day, you'll grow up and wear my old coat. Thanks to you, my dear nephew, I feel safe in the knowledge that this coat will outlive me in the world of junk. Happy bargain-hunting! Your old aunt Edgar.'

The solicitor had read out these words, his eyebrows raised in confusion. My parents were speechless; I was smiling out of the corner of my mouth. I was thirteen. Uncle Edgar, whom we hadn't heard from in years, had just died, leaving me the sum total of his possessions: his coat.

When I had grown to six feet tall, I brushed the mothballs from my uncle's cape and put it over my shoulders one December morning. It was a very windy day and the black cape flapped behind me in the maze of the flea market, the 'world of junk' the coat had not roamed through for such a long time. I was nineteen and I had six hundred francs in cash in my wallet. After haggling for some time, I left the aisles of Vernaison market with my pockets filled with two sixteenth-century paxes, those little bronze plates shaped like irons that the faithful used to kiss at communion. An hour later, I sold them on to a dealer in a café for ten times what I had paid for them. I used the money I had made to go back and buy an object which had caught my eye that morning, but had been beyond my means: a rosewood liqueur caddy with 'Lord Byron, Venezia' engraved on its copper badge.

On his trips to Venice, the poet-adventurer had the curious habit of diving into the lagoon at the Lido and swimming breaststroke up the canal to his mistress's palace. Still dripping with water, he would lie down nonchalantly on sofas covered in Fortuny fabric, open his liqueur caddy and pour himself a cognac. Tipping his head back, he would be lost in contemplation of the Settecento frescos covering the ceiling before at last kissing the beautiful lady, his lips tasting of alcohol and the salt water of the lagoon.

'… they carry the memory of their past owners.'

That same evening I poured a cognac into one of Byron's glasses and looked up at the plain white ceiling of my student bedroom. No lagoon, no clouds on the ceiling, no mistress to enliven the dull existence of a law student. But one day the ceiling would be covered in clouds and nymphs, and a fair maiden would offer me her breasts. I was sure of it.

I raise my hand to the cape's black cloth and it, too, is red hot. I think of bringing a thermometer to the shed in order to measure just how high the afternoon temperature gets. Forty-five degrees, maybe even fifty, would be my guess.

It's more than a year since I arrived here at Rivaille on the Mandragore estate. More than a year since I became the Comte de Mandragore.

II.
THE ABSENTEE

After driving for three hours and forty minutes, I parked my Jaguar in the little village square. Here I was in Rivaille. There was almost no sign of life at that time of the morning, just an old Renault 4, a Clio and a little van. I got out of the car and took some deep breaths of fresh air. It's only when you're in the countryside that you notice how polluted, stale, and, worst of all, stupefying the air in Paris is. I moved my head side to side, stretched my arms then shut the car door as I caught sight of the nearest café: La Jument Verte, with its 'Loto' and 'Tabac' signs. I headed there for a double espresso and croissants, after which I'd ask for directions to the chateau.

I pushed open the door of the bistro. The few early-morning regulars, the ones who enjoyed a little glass of white or a half-pint to help them wake up properly, turned to look at me. As I leant my elbow on the white metal bar, the owner, a round, bald, red-faced man, was straightening up from the beer pump. He stopped midway, and his chubby drinker's face froze. When I looked at the other customers I saw they were also staring at me intently. They had even put their drinks down.

'Monsieur le Comte ...' murmured the owner weakly, as he came towards me. 'We thought we'd never see you again.'

Hesitatingly, he held his hand out to me. Not knowing what else to do, I shook it, which had the effect of making him shout out, 'Martine! Come and see!'

Martine, a plump blonde woman of about fifty, appeared in the doorway of the kitchen. Her face immediately lit up in a radiant, almost ecstatic smile. 'Monsieur le Comte,' she murmured in her turn, letting go of the tea towel she was holding.

I looked back at the other customers. One of them raised his glass in my direction. His gesture was swiftly repeated by everyone in the bar in a synchronised order not unlike a Mexican wave. This was an unexpected, mad situation, and I didn't have the strength to put it right. I felt like an onlooker. A helpless onlooker, terrified, but fascinated.

'Drinks! Drinks all round!' the owner now declared excitedly. 'This is the best thing that's happened since Young Marcellin won the football pools! Go and get the '64,' he instructed his wife. 'The '64 is what this calls for!' he went on, bounding about like a dog.

Martine disappeared behind the bar, returning straight away with a bottle of 1964 vintage Clos Mandragore.

'Corkscrew!' demanded the owner in the manner of a surgeon requesting a scalpel.

His wife opened a drawer in which there were several corkscrews. Collecting corkscrews had been very fashionable a few years ago; the owner must have made a hobby of it.

'The Presto,' he said, indicating one of them. His wife held out an elegant corkscrew with arms which he applied expertly, neatly drawing out the cork with a satisfying pop.

'Monsieur le Comte, your motto, let's hear it!' cried the owner.

Swept along on the wind of panic that had sprung up with my arrival in the café, I raised my glass and declared, 'None but me!'

'None but you, Monsieur le Comte!' responded the regulars.

The Chassagne-Montrachet slipped down like velvet ambrosia, noticeably raising my pulse. Aimé-Charles de Rivaille, Comte de Mandragore, that was who I was to these people. I let them speak, making do with a nod from time to time. As I listened to them, a story gradually took shape. Four years ago, Aimé-Charles had gone to Paris to see a wine distributor but had never arrived. No one had seen him since and his car had never been found. Mélaine de Rivaille, his wife, had taken over the running of the estate and the chateau. She had not remarried.

'So where were you?' the owner asked, leaning towards me.

I turned towards the dozen people who had gathered around us. The owner's wife was refilling their glasses. I could not disappoint them, and would they believe me anyway if I told them the truth? That my name was Pierre-François Chaumont and that I had come from Paris after buying a painting at Drouot Auction House? … No, they would not believe me. I had already taken things too far.

Besides which I was a lawyer, professionally trained in the art of using words. It would not be the first time that I had forced myself to talk nonsense. It was just that I had never before had to do so on my own account. I had never had to work without a safety net. It was like bungee-jumping without elastic. I decided to jump; it was too good an opportunity to miss, even more exciting than an auction. I had never experienced such a frisson. I was about to try something out on these people to see if they would take the bait.

'Dédé,' interrupted his wife, giving him a discreet nudge with her elbow, 'perhaps the count doesn't want to talk about it. These things are personal.'

'I had an accident,' I told them, in the tone of one whose only desire is to unburden himself.

'I knew it,' the owner immediately exclaimed.

An accident. A car accident, there, that was what had happened, a car accident; at least that's what I had been told because I couldn't remember anything about it. I had woken up without any papers and with no memory in a convalescent home in the suburbs of Paris. That's where I had been looked after. The care had been excellent and a few weeks ago my memory had started to return little by little thanks to electric shock treatment. I was not entirely recovered, and although, of course, I recognised the people around me, I couldn't quite remember their names. Everything would come back but it would take time. It was at my request that my doctor had agreed that I could return alone to Mandragore to confront reality. He had lent me his car – that was his fine Jaguar parked over there.

'Amnesia!' exclaimed the owner. 'We saw a programme about that on the telly last week.'

How could I have fooled them so easily?

'And what did they say at the chateau?' asked the customer with the half-pint.

'At the chateau ...' I murmured. 'I haven't been to the chateau yet ...'

The owner's wife looked horrified and put her hand over her mouth. '*Mon Dieu*, Madame Mélaine doesn't know yet!' she gasped.

'So we're the first to know!' cried the large bald man.

The question of my papers was quickly dealt with.

'And you don't have your papers with you?'

'He was attacked by thugs – those criminals take everything, even identity papers.'

'You know, they're worth a lot of money, identity papers.'

'I thought they couldn't be faked.'

'It's the serial numbers that are important. I saw a Jean-Pierre Pernaut documentary about it.'

The mention of the famous journalist brought the argument to a close.

'You look well, at least,' confirmed the owner. 'And you haven't changed … Well, perhaps your hair's a bit shorter.'

'That will be the hospital barber; they use clippers,' grumbled one of the customers, before looking in my direction for confirmation.

'Yes, yes, it's all a bit military,' I replied, whereas, in fact, I paid one hundred and sixty euros a month to have my hair cut at a chic salon on Avenue Georges V.

It is easy to convince people who want to believe. You just have to tell them what they want to hear. That's it, there's nothing else to it. The words are already formed inside them; all you have to do is say them like a magic spell to produce the desired effect. Nature had decreed that I should look exactly like the man who had disappeared, and no one dared challenge what I told them. On the contrary, they had drunk in my words with even more relish than they had the Montrachet '64. And now that I was leaving the café, they were all watching me with the look of those who are the proud keepers of a great secret.

'So we're the first to know!'

Those words kept going round in my head, distant and intoxicating, like an annoying earworm.

For several minutes I had been sitting, eyes closed, with my forehead against the steering wheel. Could the solitude and silence of this dirt track help me come to a decision? I had just gone through the strangest experience of my life and I almost wondered whether it had actually happened. Yes – it had. On my journey from Paris, I had run through just about every answer I might receive to my questions about the painting. Every answer except the one I got, without asking a single question.

Within my web of lies there was nonetheless a grain of truth. And if I had found it easy to spin a yarn, it's because it was based on fact. The convalescent home was not a product of my imagination but belonged to Dr Martin Baretti, a perfectly affable man but with something about him that suggested his life was more complicated than it first seemed. He had called upon my services a few months earlier to patent a new form of electric shock therapy.

If my passion for objects created an instant connection with fellow collectors, my day job also sometimes made me the recipient of confidences. Lawyers and bankers are the custodians of people's lives, and sometimes their clients treat them like confessors. Because of their professions they are seen as trustworthy, and less intimidating than men of the cloth, who in any case stopped hearing confession half a century ago.

Once, while contemplating an engraving of a young woman who had been hanged, a collector standing alongside me had admitted to a predilection for bondage, tying up his partner until she was on the verge of passing out. He had even taken an assortment of Polaroids out of his wallet to show me. Dr Baretti, meanwhile, was living a double life: one as a married father of two, and the other with the young male lover he had set up in a charming pied-à-terre in the Marais. When I went to see an electric-shock-therapy demonstration at his clinic, I had noticed how close the doctor appeared to be to the young blond nurse named Jean-Stéphane. Dr Baretti caught me looking at his partner and smiled.

'Yes, Maître Chaumont, I'm perfectly homosexual,' he confirmed on our return to his office.

I began to wonder how it was possible to be 'perfectly' homosexual when you had a wife and two daughters, but remembered the doctor had already used that adverb a good half-dozen times. Why on earth had the man chosen to tell me? Perhaps because one day it might be useful to me.

*

I was ashamed of my behaviour. Ashamed of what I was turning into: an impostor playing on the credulity of good honest people. There was no getting away from it: I was no better than those cult leaders who prey on the weak-minded and lost; I had always despised such people, yet here I was behaving in exactly the same way. Maybe I was even worse than them. I had nothing to sell, no religion, no one-way ticket to another planet. Unless I was already unconsciously plotting my own departure as the crowd looked on, enthralled.

And yet, despite being horrified by my own lies, I was also starting to see things another way: I hadn't left Paris by chance; I wasn't here by chance; I didn't resemble this man by chance. What had happened since my discovery of the portrait was no fluke. I was following my destiny. Anything I might say to disabuse these people would be to go against my fate. A door was opening before me; I had only to step through it or go back the way I had come.

I turned to look at the pastel. Through the bubble wrap I could see the face of the man in the powdered wig. The portrait was offering me the chance of a lifetime: the chance to become someone else. It was an opportunity to do something crazy which would never come my way again. My train of thought was interrupted when my mobile phone rang. 'Charlotte' came up on the screen. I turned it off to shut it up. Maybe I would never turn it back on again.

At the start of the dirt track there was a sign, fixed to a centuries-old tree, which read, 'Welcome to the Mandragore Estate'. Those words stencilled in red on a white background delivered a mild blow to my solar plexus.

All around me vines spread out over the hills as far as the eye could see before disappearing into the summer haze. I noticed that at the foot of each vine there was a curious cylinder of rusty metal pierced with holes, like a sort of miner's lamp planted vertically in the soil, very near the roots. It looked like a system for keeping the roots at a stable temperature in winter. I couldn't help wondering who had filed the patent application. It must have been a profitable invention since there was one for every vine.

Apart from some crows flying around in the distance there was no one about but me. Yes, me, Pierre-François Chaumont, the lawyer. And as I was repeating my name, I reflected that we always act in the same manner when faced with important decisions in our lives: during the few minutes preceding the decision, we seem bound to do the opposite of what we eventually decide. We try to convince ourselves one last time that there is another option. We want to think there is a simpler, more reassuring path. A better alternative. Yes, a few seconds before we embrace the inevitable, we comfort ourselves with illusions. We can't help it. 'I'm only going to the chateau so that I can meet Mélaine de Rivaille and explain everything to her,' I told myself. 'I am not Aimé-Charles, I am Pierre-François. Pierre-François Chaumont. I am a Paris lawyer specialising in industrial processes, patents, all sorts of patents, fibre optics, evolutionary microchips, ball bearings, Durit.'

The house appeared before me as I rounded a hedge. An immense building with high walls of light-coloured stone, reflected in the water of the moat. I knew exactly where I was. I had seen the chateau that morning on the internet. Yet, as the images had been taken from a helicopter, the photos had not conveyed the magnificence of the building.

The wooden bridge made no sound as I crossed it. I had expected it to creak under my weight but it didn't. The wind created light ripples on the heavy green water and once again I saw a snapshot from my past. This time it was the wrinkled skin of the warm milk Céline used to make cakes with in my childhood. I went into the first courtyard. There was a group of about twenty people standing by one of the towers talking quietly to each other as they unfolded maps and brochures.

'Here he is!' cried a blonde woman, pointing at me.

I smiled at her but immediately spread my hands in a gesture of helplessness. No, I was not their guide.

'Want one?' a man in yellow shorts asked me. He had taken me for a tourist and was holding out a packet of white marshmallows. 'Made in the USA' said the packet in red and blue letters. He must have brought them with him. Where was he from?

'California,' he replied.

Then as I chewed the big white marshmallow, he explained that he still loved France, that the politicians could squabble with each other over world problems, but he, James Fridman, didn't care. He loved France, and burgundy. And as for the war, corruption, the UN and the journalists … 'Fuck them all!' he declared with the air of someone skilfully summarising his argument.

'Fuck them all,' I agreed in my turn, swallowing the sugary, fluffy paste.

A young man with a blond crew cut hurried over to the group. He was carrying a large guidebook. He introduced himself and asked the group to excuse his lateness, first in French, then in English. James Fridman gave him a friendly pat on the shoulder and offered him his bag of marshmallows, which the young man refused with a shake of the head. It was time for me to interrupt.

'Please excuse me,' I said. 'I'm looking for Mélaine de Rivaille.'

'The Comtesse doesn't take part in the guided tours,' said the young man, looking irritated.

'I'm not part of the guided tour. I have come to see her,' I replied.

The young man was put out. He mumbled something about the estate management and a 'Monsieur Henri' to whom I would have to introduce myself, but who was busy with the silverware. Through the windows of what must have been the drawing room, I caught the eye of an old man carrying silver dishes on a tray. He froze, and the tray fell from his hands, crashing onto the tiled floor. A moment later the same old man was standing, breathless, before me.

'Monsieur … Oh Monsieur,' he murmured.

He did not leave me time to work out how to reply before saying softly, 'Madame is in the rose garden.'

I followed his gaze and found I was looking at one of the tourist signs, which pointed to the rose garden with a purple arrow.

A hectare of roses running either side of narrow pathways paved with white stone. The extraordinary rose garden had a large, weather-beaten information board which told visitors everything they needed to know. I skimmed over it, taking in the occasional name or number: one hundred and forty rose varieties, more than three hundred individual rosebushes. Each one was listed with the name of its group and breeder and the date of its creation. I scrolled down: Triomphe de France, centifolia, Cariou, 1823. Duke of Burgundy, hybrid perpetual, Elliot, 1967. Pierre de Ronsard, modern hybrid, Meilland, 1987. Lady Mélaine, centifolia, Silver, gift from Arthur McEllie, 1997 – Winner, Belles d'Europe '98; crowned Rose of France '99; named one of the centifolias of the millennium in 2000.

Where was Lady Mélaine among all these hundreds of flowers? Where was the rose? Where was the woman? I could see no one amongst the tall stems and bushes; the old retainer must have been mistaken. I scanned all the labels: Gloire des Comtes, Unique Panachée, Sœur de Neige, Jeanne de France, Impératrice Mauve … As I weaved my way along the paths, the abundance of names and corollas began to make me feel dizzy.

Lady Mélaine. A centifolia, according to the detailed description on the little marker placed at its foot. Its many accolades were also listed in italics. The bush should produce around forty flowers with fleshy petals, crumpled as if they had just got out of bed. They were a very pale shade of orange. The biggest petals faded almost to white at their tips, while those in the middle were more intensely coloured throughout. I brought my lips and nose to a flower and a sweet, peppery scent wafted up in the morning heat. I closed my eyes. When I opened them again a moment later, I saw a shape move a few rows away.

It was definitely a woman, there among the roses. I made out a pale dress in a faded sea-green colour. I walked to the end of the stone pathway. Yes, it was a strappy dress, the kind with buttons down the front.

Her legs were bare and she wore white ballet pumps. She was leaning over a rosebush holding a wicker basket in which the faded roses she had just dead-headed were visible. Long locks of hair fell in front of her face. They were the shade of blond that's almost red – Venetian blond, as they used to call it in the eighteenth century, after the way the girls of La Serenissima dyed their hair. But the colour of the hair I was looking at had not come out of a bottle. The rose that carried her name was a similar shade; that was why an American admirer had presented it to the mistress of Mandragore.

She lifted her head and swiftly tucked her hair behind her ears. Mélaine de Rivaille. She had pale, almost white skin, with just a scattering of freckles on her nose. Even from this distance, I could make out the brightness of her eyes and above all of her lips, which were a deep red colour that surely owed nothing to lipstick. The delicacy of her features continued down the slender line of her neck towards her chest. Beneath the slight rise in the cotton, I could see she wasn't wearing a bra. She leant forwards to look at a flower and her dress gaped open, revealing her small breasts. How old was Mélaine de Rivaille? Thirty-five, maybe thirty-seven?

She took off her right shoe, checked the sole, then removed the left and placed both in the basket with the rose heads. Then she began walking towards the next bush, her bare feet against the warm stone. The cotton dress hugged her thighs as she moved. I couldn't stop looking at her long bare legs and white feet advancing over the stones. She stopped and I looked up at her face.

She stared at me. Her whole being, until now all movement, became perfectly still. Her mouth hung slightly open, her eyes were locked on mine. Pale green, like the dress.

It wasn't my imagination, a brief moan really had just emerged from her chest, and here it was again, stronger, as though she couldn't hold it back, her heart suddenly beating too fast and the oxygen struggling to keep up with the flow of blood. I, too, felt a wave of emotion flooding over me. My heart was thumping at the sight of this wild-eyed woman who could not speak, but only let out these little cries.

She dropped the basket and it bounced on the ground, scattering rose heads all over the slabs.

She flung herself at me with surprising force. Then she looked at me without a sound. We were both dumbstruck: for her it was the shock of seeing me again; for me the emotion of meeting her for the first time.

Finally, she regained the power of speech

'It's you, it's you,' she murmured and squeezed me so tightly I lost my balance.

We fell together onto the baking-hot stone. She fixed me with a pale stare, her eyes shining with tears. Between breaths, she said the words again: 'It's you, it's you.'

The straps of her dress had slipped off her shoulders but she hadn't noticed. Her hair had fallen over her face and I placed my hands on either side of her head. I could feel her hips against me through the thin cotton dress, see her bare ankles and feet resting on the path. I closed my eyes and all I could feel was her breath and the quivering of her body. She brought her face close and pressed her lips to mine. Neither of us could complete the kiss, nor even start it. We were joined together, as if resuscitating one another. Struggling for air, I pulled away.

'It's me, it's me, it's me, it's me!' I said, having finally recovered my breath.

I couldn't stop now.

My eyes had grown used to the darkness of the room. There was enough daylight filtering through the heavy velvet curtains for me to make out a bedside table, a telephone, a chest of drawers, a *globe de mariée* and pictures on the walls. I was lying on the bed, still dressed, although my jacket was on the armchair. Had I fainted? It was perfectly possible. I started to get up when I felt a burning-hot hand on my chest. I turned my head. Mélaine was lying by my side looking at me. She had adjusted the straps of her dress. I instantly remembered the shock of the feeling of her body against mine, her imploring gaze and her uneven breathing. Yes, I had fainted, I was sure of it now.

I stared at the stranger I had taken in my arms who now lay peacefully at my side on the bed cover. I could not take my eyes off her. Never had a woman appeared more beautiful, more desirable, or more closely attuned to me. We seemed to have raced through all the normal stages of seduction in a few seconds.

We lay like that for a long time, neither moving nor

speaking. I wanted to say into the silence of the room, 'I love you.' I love you. How long was it since I had spoken those words? In fact, had I ever spoken them? I was starting to wonder.

'I can explain everything,' I said in a low voice.

She nodded gravely. I was about to begin explaining my amnesia, but she put her finger on my lips. Her breath quickened, she removed her sea-green dress and white pants. I watched her, excited but terrified. She slipped on top of me and began to undo the buttons of my shirt. I helped her and was soon also undressed.

Now we were both naked in the dark, gently lit by the sun behind the velvet curtains. I took her in my arms. She moved herself further up and put her hands on my shoulders. Now her breasts were level with my face, her hair was falling forwards and I parted it, smoothing it with my fingers.

'I haven't been unfaithful to you,' she murmured.

Now it was my turn to look at her gravely, and the words came easily to me: 'I love you, I will love you for ever.'

We kissed passionately, before her lips left mine and moved down along my neck. I opened my eyes and looked up at the bedroom ceiling. It was white. But what I saw there were the most beautiful clouds that had ever graced any landscape. And far far away, on one of them, I saw a figure disappearing into the distance in a black cape until he was nothing more than a speck, which eventually disappeared. My previous life had ceased to exist. Nothing had ever existed except Mélaine de Rivaille and Mandragore.

'We looked everywhere for you, everywhere ... Why couldn't we find you in that clinic?'

'I don't know,' I murmured.

And we fell silent. Then Mélaine cuddled up to me and we stayed in each other's arms for a while.

We had made love and I hadn't had the strength to tell my story of amnesia. It had taken me several hours to find the courage to lie. Deep down I would rather have told her the truth, that she had mistaken me for her vanished husband and that I did want to replace him. I wanted to live at Mandragore with her and to love her. That was all I wanted, to tell her morning and night that I loved her and to make love to her as often as she wanted. I had never made love like that. I had never loved. But I was obliged to lie, to tell her the story of amnesia, the clinic, Dr Baretti, the only real part of the story.

'I'll bring you my medical file. I'll go back to Paris and get it,' I had insisted, partly to convince myself.

'You never used to smoke,' she said gently.

'I don't smoke,' I protested.

'I smelt it on your clothes,' she said, smiling.

Was the magical interlude where anything was possible about to dissolve? There would be more and more questions, and each would be more specific than the last. I was in danger of tripping myself up over the details;

I needed to snap out of my intoxicated state as soon as possible, get a grip and stay alert. I could not lose the love of my life, or rather, of my new life.

'Dr Baretti smokes, and I began to smoke with him. There is so little to do in the clinic ...' I added wearily.

'Give me a cigarette,' she said.

Then my eye fell on my jacket and I immediately considered what was in the pockets. There was my wallet and my papers – identity card, credit card, car registration, car insurance and social security card. I didn't have a packet of cigarettes but there was my tortoiseshell cigarette case with the Venice scene. I decided to risk everything by taking it out and proffering it to Mélaine.

'It's beautiful,' she said. And immediately added, 'It's not yours.'

'No, it's Dr Baretti's.'

'Like the Jaguar. Your doctor has lent you so many things!'

Mélaine was studying me through narrowed eyes, lighting her cigarette with a faint smile.

'Is he gay?'

'Yes, he is!' I said, surprised.

'You were always attractive to men,' she said, exhaling. 'Don't you remember?'

'No, I don't. Tell me about it.'

She fetched a crystal ashtray from the chest of drawers and came over to the bed. I touched her cheek lovingly. 'You'll have to tell me. I can't remember everything yet.'

Mélaine was thirty-seven and I was forty-three. We had met twelve years earlier at a winemakers' conference in Dijon. Mélaine Gaulthier was a young journalist noted for a feature on François Mitterrand's walks in the Morvan mountains, and her latest project was a piece on burgundy producers for the *Figaro* summer supplement. Clos Mandragore was one of the vineyards she had decided to focus on. Mélaine had noticed me at the start of the conference, and I couldn't take my eyes off her. When I got up on the little stage to promote Mandragore wines, I took the opportunity to ask her to join me. I claimed I needed 'an innocent tongue' to try the wine and chose Mélaine before I even knew her name.

She told me that the expression 'innocent tongue' made a frisson of excitement run through her. That same evening, back at the chateau, we took that frisson further. My father, the Comte de Mandragore, declared that 'the prettiest mandrake has just sprung up on the estate'. The next morning, I asked Mélaine to stay with me for ever and be my wife.

'Everything you see here belongs to you,' I told her.

She asked me to give her a week to go back to Paris, abandon her *Figaro* assignment and break up with her boyfriend. In the event, four days were enough.

The only fly in the ointment of this passionate love story was that this most beautiful of mandrakes was unable to have children. A cloud had hung over us for a few years until one evening we eventually accepted that we would be the last of the Rivaille-Mandragores. The line that could be traced back to the twelfth century would die out in the twenty-first.

'Nine centuries is a pretty good innings,' I concluded.

This near-millennium of family history was part of our daily life. We often went to look at our ancestors in the portrait gallery. The earliest were little illuminated watercolours on parchment, and all that was missing was one of the two of us. We had opted to have an oil painting done by a local artist to make a change from the recent portraits, all photographs by the Harcourt studio.

'Isn't there another one that's missing?' I asked, interrupting Mélaine's account.

'Yes, there is … So that's one thing you haven't forgotten.'

'Who is it of?'

The question which had been burning on my lips since that day in room eight at Drouot Auction House would at last be answered.

*

Louis-Auguste, Comte de Mandragore, known as 'the absentee' after absenting himself from his own life. He had been a friend of Louis XVI and shared the King's passion for locksmithing. During the Terror, Louis-Auguste was arrested in Paris and imprisoned for several weeks. He escaped and, after witnessing the terrifying spectacle of the sovereign's execution, went back to the provinces without a sou to his name. Fearful of returning to Burgundy and Mandragore, he took refuge in a little village in the Auvergne where he worked as a blacksmith and locksmith, thereby abandoning his wife, children and chateau. No one questioned his metalwork skills at the forge. Claiming his birth certificate and apprenticeship papers had been lost in a fire at the guild archives, he took on the name of his former master blacksmith: Chaumont. As Mélaine continued to tell the tale of Auguste Chaumont, my throat tightened and my head began to spin.

My father had once asked a genealogist to carry out some research on the Chaumont family tree. The line mysteriously stopped in the late eighteenth century with a locksmith in the Auvergne: Auguste Chaumont.

The thirteenth Comte de Mandragore, my ancestor.

Now I knew. All that remained was to do as the first of the Chaumonts had done before me and disappear. After all, making oneself scarce ran in the family.

'I'm hungry,' she said, stubbing out her third cigarette. 'Are you?'

'Yes.'

Mélaine got up and wrapped a dressing gown around herself, sea green like the cotton dress, like her eyes.

'There must be some veal left in the kitchen,' she murmured, doing up her belt. 'I won't be long.'

These few words made my heart thump almost as hard as holding her in my arms had done. If we could exchange such anodyne phrases as these, then yes, I was her husband; yes, I had always been here. Yes, this woman was my wife. There was no doubt about it. I felt the urge to get up, head down to the kitchen, hold her and tell her how amazing it was that there was leftover veal in the fridge, that this would be the best meal of my entire life: two slices of cold veal with a dab of mayonnaise, eaten straight off the waxed tablecloth in the kitchen at Mandragore. But I didn't know where the kitchen was. If I left the bedroom, I wouldn't be able to find Mélaine.

I knew I had to make the most of being left alone there.

'I need to call Dr Baretti,' I said to myself. 'Now.' I got out of bed, took my phone out of my jacket pocket and turned it on. A message flashed up on the screen: twenty-two voicemails. I scrolled through the numbers: Charlotte, Charlotte, Chevrier, Chevrier, Foscarini F1 Team, Charlotte, Chevrier, Tajan Auction House, Expert Associates, Vaudhier and Partners, Chevrier, Chevrier, Charlotte, Samuel Antiques, Marchandeau Books, Orange Customer Service, Charlotte, Heraldic Bookshop, Charlotte, Chevrier and finally two missed calls from an unknown number.

'This is a message for Monsieur Pierre-François Chaumont. This is Lieutenant Masquatier calling from the police station in the seventeenth arrondissement in Paris. I'm contacting you because we have received a missing persons report filed by your wife, Charlotte Chaumont, and your business partner, Monsieur Alain Chevrier. These individuals have had no contact from you for twenty-four hours and they're concerned for your welfare, Monsieur. I should point out that no search operation has been launched at this time. You're an adult; you have the right to come and go as you please. Nevertheless, we're trying to make contact with you at the request of your loved ones. If for any reason you are unable to contact them or us …'

The message was cut off there. No doubt I could hear the rest in the next voicemail. I decided not to listen to it.

Soon they would begin looking for me. If I made a call from this phone, it could easily be traced. Having worked on broadcast technology patents, I knew that as soon as a call was made anywhere in France, the number was automatically logged on the servers. I opened my contacts and went to the folder for clients with names beginning with B. While looking up the doctor's number on my mobile, I picked up the landline phone on the bedside table, all the time keeping an ear out for Mélaine. The house was silent. I dialled the number.

'Dr Baretti? Maître Chaumont here. Tell me, Dr Baretti, are you still perfectly homosexual? … I'm sorry too, Doctor … sorry for what I'm about to do, but I'm afraid I've no choice, and you've no choice but to help me.'

There wasn't a single place to stop on either Rue des Archives or Rue Sainte-Croix-de-la-Bretonnerie. I couldn't leave the car double-parked since a parking ticket would ruin my plan, so I decided to park at the town hall. Feeling a bit paranoid, I tried to conceal my identity from the surveillance cameras by putting on the dark glasses I had found that morning at the chateau in the lost property drawer.

I had seen the terror in Mélaine's eyes when I told her I was leaving Mandragore. I understood why and took her in my arms, saying, 'I will come back this time.'

'I don't want this just to have been a dream,' she told me. 'I don't want to wake and find I am alone.'

'Neither do I; I never want to wake up again.'

She may have wondered what I meant but she did not question me. She watched me walk away towards the gates of the chateau. I turned to look at her one last time as she stood at the bottom of the steps. The old retainer who had dropped the tray of silver a few days earlier went over to her and I saw Mélaine put her hand on his arm and hold it a long time, in a gesture of friendship and possibly because she felt faint.

'This is a message for Maître Chaumont. It's Lieutenant Masquatier again. Your phone operator has confirmed that you have listened to your messages, unless your phone has been stolen and is now in the hands of a third party ...'

I snapped the phone shut immediately in horror. They knew that I had listened to my messages. I would have to get rid of the phone as soon as possible. I placed it on the first public bench I came to and hid behind a tree to see if anyone would steal it. A young man in a tracksuit went past. His gaze fell on the phone then he took his headphones out. He looked to left and right, sat down, stayed still for a few seconds then got up and walked quickly away. The telephone had gone. I wasn't worried that he would drop it off at the lost property. I was relieved that the last link to my old life and to the endless questions from the police officer was now being carried away in the pocket of his tracksuit.

I was looking for a club called Thomas l'imposteur. After going up and down the street several times with no luck, I went into a boutique that sold tight trousers and hiking boots and offered a piercing service. A young man in a close-fitting white T-shirt with 'porn star' emblazoned across the chest welcomed me with a smile.

'Hello, I need to go to … this address, but I can't see the sign anywhere,' I said, holding out my piece of paper.

The boy's smile widened and his eyes brightened. 'You go into the courtyard. It's on the left as you go outside. There's no entry code for the door.'

As I was leaving he called out in a friendly way, 'But you'd better knock; it's usually closed at this time!'

He had assumed I was gay, reminding me of the way I was sometimes taken for a Freemason. Like all good collectors I was interested in Masonic symbolism and in the objects the brotherhood had produced over the centuries. My interest sometimes led me to visit the specialist bookshops on Rue Puteaux or Rue Cadet. When I asked knowledgeable questions, the sales assistants would fetch books for me and address me as a friend. I had been a Freemason by adoption, now I was gay by adoption, and as I walked along the street I felt the powerful presence of my uncle following me. He had died much too early and had never known the gay scene in the Marais. 'This *quartier* would have finished him off,' I thought. 'He wouldn't even have had a cape to leave me.' I pushed open the heavy door and entered the paved courtyard. At the back on the left the red metal door had presumably led in previous times to the building's coal cellars. Now there was a bell and a little laminated notice: 'Thomas … l'imposteur'.

I rang but there was no answer and I was about to knock when the door opened.

'So it's you,' said Dr Baretti wearily.

He was very at home in the large room with the tiled floor and was wearing one of the light three-piece suits that I had seen him in previously. It seemed to me his grey hair was shorter than usual. At the back of the room I noticed a bar and sofas, then a spiral staircase leading to the basement. On one of the sofas I recognised Jean-Stéphane whom I nodded to. He turned away and continued to drink his peppermint cordial. Dr Baretti went to sit down beside him and indicated that I should take the white leather ottoman, which I did, sinking down almost to the floor.

'Is this what you call a back room?' I asked to break the silence.

'I don't believe you're here to perfect your knowledge of gay culture, are you now, Maître?' Dr Baretti replied coldly.

I agreed with a movement of my hand that, indeed, that was not why I was here.

'Before we go any further, I have to tell you I find this absolutely disgraceful.'

'I would have to agree with you,' I replied calmly.

Again, the three of us looked at each other in silence. Dr Baretti was right, it was absolutely disgraceful. I had called him to let him know that I would tell his wife and daughters about Jean-Stéphane unless he provided me with all necessary proof that I had been in his clinic for the last four years, under the name of Aimé-Charles de Rivaille, Comte de Mandragore.

'It took me all night to do this,' said the doctor, opening

a red file. 'Here is a real fake file. I falsified my computer records for the last four years; for you I have even falsified a police report. Have you brought the photos?'

I showed him the photos I had taken in a photo booth at the metro station. My hair was a mess, I looked distraught. 'If you're claiming to be the victim of an accident, don't appear in your best suit. You need to look as bad as possible,' he had told me the day before. Politely, I pointed out that I had gone as far as to add a bruise to my temple with a make-up crayon bought that morning at a service station. He glared at me and snatched the photos from me before asking Jean-Stéphane if he would mind getting a pair of scissors and a tube of glue.

'I like the reference to Cocteau,' I said, as the doctor carefully glued my photographs in place.

As he did not reply, I went on, 'For the name of the club ...'

'You like Cocteau?' Jean-Stéphane asked me.

'Yes, very much,' I replied.

'I suppose that redeems you slightly ...' murmured Baretti.

A few minutes later, the photos were drying on the seventy-two-page medical file.

'I never want to hear anything about you ever again,' Baretti told me, as he accompanied me back to the metal door.

'I don't want to hear anything about me ever again either.'

He nodded and I left the courtyard.

Outside, the street was sunny, young people were walking hand in hand, and I was no longer frightened. I was Aimé-Charles de Rivaille. It said so in the file, on the page headed 'Memory recovery': 'The man named Jean since his arrival this morning claims to be called Aimé-Charles de Rivaille from Burgundy.'

News in brief

A lawyer has gone missing from the seventeenth arrondissement in Paris. The family and colleagues of Maître Pierre-François Chaumont say they have not heard from him in almost two weeks. His car, a Jaguar XJS, and some personal effects are also missing. An intellectual-property specialist, he had recently been working as the lead lawyer on a sensitive case concerning a new engine part used in Formula 1 cars. Police have not ruled out any line of enquiry.

Courtroom dispatches

A major upset in the small world of Formula 1. After the disappearance three months ago of Parisian lawyer Pierre-François Chaumont, who had been working on a dispute over a new Durit system (BN-657), police yesterday carried out dawn raids on the premises of rival teams Laren and Foscarini. An official source revealed that the police have not excluded the possibility of a link between the lawyer's disappearance and industrial espionage.

OUTBURST

Franck Massoulier, a highly respected fluid-mechanics researcher within Formula 1, caused a disturbance at a Speed & Passion show at the Porte de Versailles Exhibition Centre last night. Massoulier grabbed the microphone during a media presentation of the new Foscarini engines and accused the show's guest of honour, Gianni Foscarini, 96, of having ordered the kidnap and assassination of his lawyer, Pierre-François Chaumont, from whom nothing has been heard in the past eight months (see previous issues). Monsieur Massoulier, who is bilingual, used the language of Dante to launch a tirade of insults at Gianni Foscarini and attempted to physically attack the elderly man before security guards were able to restrain him.

SENTENCING

Massoulier, the engineer and top Formula 1 figure who insulted Gianni Foscarini and his group some months ago (see previous issues), has been ordered to pay damages of two thousand euros plus interest to the Foscarini group for slander, defamation and obscenity. There is still no news of lawyer Maître Chaumont, whose mysterious disappearance provides the background to this case. Police have abandoned the line of enquiry linking Chaumont's disappearance to his professional activities, due to lack of evidence. The focus has now turned to his contacts within the art world. Maître Chaumont's name appears in the professional diary of auctioneer Paul Pétillon, charged six months ago with handling stolen goods.

The Cranach Affair

'Crooks, yes. Murderers, no!' This was the Attorney General's verdict on the accused. The auctioneer Paul Pétillon and antiques dealers Carpentier, Beauchon and Victurian were questioned all morning about lawyer Maître Chaumont, who has been missing for almost a year, and with whom they have all had past dealings. The criminal investigation linking Chaumont to the 'Cranach Affair' has been dropped.

The Chaumont Affair

Regrettably, this headline is misleading. There is no Chaumont affair, none at all, but we would like to take this opportunity to pay tribute to the Parisian lawyer who has now been missing for a year. Chaumont was a patents specialist and for a time his disappearance was linked to the world of Formula 1 – specifically, there was speculation he might have become an innocent victim of the industrial-espionage war that has plagued the sport. This line of enquiry came to a dead end. Police investigated Chaumont's private life, looking for evidence of the sexual misdemeanours or money worries that often lie behind uncharacteristic disappearances. Nothing. The most recent line of enquiry attempted to link the lawyer's disappearance to the art world. His name and mobile phone number appeared in the professional or private diaries of a number of auctioneers and antiques dealers, some of whom were convicted in the 'Cranach Affair' (see previous issues). An art-lover, according to his friends and family, Pierre-François Chaumont knew the antiquarians in a strictly professional capacity and only communicated with them with regard to his own collections. Those close to him describe Chaumont as having been depressed and obsessive in the months leading up to his disappearance, which sadly opens up the possibility that he may have taken his own life. It is hard to avoid comparisons with a missing-persons case we documented two years ago, that of Henri Dalmier, the Ministry of Foreign Affairs official not seen at his place of work or residence for the past twenty-five months and two weeks. Our thoughts are with the families of these two men at this very difficult time. For those left behind, learning the worst might even provide some relief from their ongoing anguish. There are between 12,000 and 15,000 disappearances every year in France, of which around 80 per cent will be explained – runaways, debt avoidance, suicide, depression, murder or an accident – while the remaining 20 per cent remain a total mystery. That's between 2,500 and 3,000 people a year who disappear without a trace. This magazine is determined not to forget them.

That was the last time the press did me the honour of writing about me. Though no full-length articles worthy of the name had been dedicated to my 'disappearance', I came across these brief accounts while browsing the crime sections. They are taken from *Le Parisien* and *Le Nouveau*

Détective, the investigative magazine that kept up the story of the vain efforts to trace me longer than the rest. It was this magazine that likened my disappearance to that of a Foreign Affairs official. I don't know whether Henri Dalmier ever resurfaced; I haven't looked into it. Over the course of this year, from my home in the depths of Burgundy, it's myself I've been trying to learn about as I browse the online newspapers. They thought I committed suicide. In a way, they weren't altogether wrong.

One evening I went into Rivaille and slipped into the telephone box in the market square, making sure that no one had seen me. I picked up the receiver and dialled my Paris number. I wanted to hear Charlotte's voice one last time. I wasn't planning to speak to her, I just wanted to listen. The phone rang for a long time but there was no reply. The sound must have reached up to the crystal of my chandelier just as Charlotte's strident cries had done a year earlier.

Then, as I had tried one number from my past, I rang another. What could be more natural than to call the friend who had been part of my life for twenty years? Chevrier. I had no intention of speaking to him either, but to hear him say 'Hello?' down the line several times would fill me with pleasure. The idea that I would be on the other end and that he would probably suspect that it was me would add to the illicit thrill.

This time the phone only rang twice and the 'Hello?' that followed hit me like a lightning bolt.

It was Charlotte. At twenty to midnight at Chevrier's house. What was she doing there?

'Hello?' she repeated.

She had picked up the phone and answered with the nonchalance of someone who belonged there. And where was the telephone? On a table, a chest of drawers, at the bedside? I tried to recall how the various items of furniture were arranged but couldn't quite remember.

'Hello?'

Her affair with Chevrier must have been going on for years. Years during which he had been telling me about his affair with the wife of another man … And that man had been me. Chevrier had never stopped loving Charlotte. She had made her life with the richer, smarter partner whilst at the same time leading another life with the one who played the role so brilliantly as my number two, my 'assistant', as certain of our clients liked to say.

'We spoke to your assistant, Maître.' 'My partner,' I corrected them. In fact he was neither partner, nor assistant; he was a lying snake consorting with a viper as soon as my back was turned. Their two bodies must have writhed in pleasure together at the weekend when I was off at the auction house raising the bidding. That was how their guilty coupling must have come about. 'My passion will have helped theirs,' I thought. Now it seemed so obvious. How could I have been so blind? Like Charlotte, Chevrier and all the others when they were looking at my portrait. The evidence was right in front of them, as it was right in front of me and yet we had seen nothing. We did not want to see anything. My wife was as invisible to me as I was to her. That phone call and the voice at the other end were just what I needed. They erased all the doubt, remorse and guilt I had been experiencing even up to this evening. I thanked Charlotte for not seeing the resemblance between me and the figure in the painting; and she could thank me for not having loved her enough for all those years. I had left the way clear for her.

After I hung up, I forced myself to contemplate the next logical step, the marriage of Charlotte and Chevrier. There was nothing to stop them marrying soon. What would become of my antiques? My study? It was the first time the thought had occurred to me. My collections, so dear to my heart, were now alone and had been abandoned by their master for several months. Yet, although I could not think of a way to get them back, I felt they were safe for now in the apartment. But they wouldn't be if those two set up home together. They would sell my collections and use the proceeds to take a round-the-world trip, I was sure of it. I would have to come up with a solution and was surprised to find myself invoking St Anthony, the patron saint of lost things. 'You must help me get my things back,' I implored him, without knowing what I would be able to do for him in return.

A few days later, Mélaine and I went to the police station for us both to sign the letter of mutual recognition making my return official.

'This is the first time I've had to go to the police station,' I said as we went in.

'The second,' corrected Commander Briard with a smile. 'Don't you remember?'

'Aimé still has some blanks,' said Mélaine gently.

'Yes, of course,' murmured the policeman, as if he had committed a faux pas.

'When was the other time?' I asked.

'The Davier brothers,' replied the commander, smiling again.

Apparently, one night, almost ten years ago, I had been out and about in Mandragore with my shotgun, looking for a fox. It had been wrecking the chateau's flower beds for several weeks. In the forest I had come across the Davier brothers. Martial and Noël had also been after the fox, but not to kill it with a shotgun. On the contrary, they wanted to kill it more gently and sell it to the taxidermist.

The Daviers were always in on all the local scams and whenever there was a burglary in the area, the first port of call for the police was always the breaker's yard at Le Pivert, the only property officially owned by the brothers and inherited from their father.

That night, the cash machine at the national savings bank in Chassanier, the little town not far from Rivaille, had been broken into. Two men had made off with quite a considerable haul. Witnesses had recounted that the two men, glimpsed in headlights, appeared to be redheads. The police had immediately recognised a description of the Davier brothers, the men who were poaching on my land. They were arrested the next day and, when I heard of it, I went to the police station to say that at the time of the break-in, the brothers had been with me in the forest. The Daviers had not yet said anything, since mentioning the taxidermist would only have added to their woes. My spontaneous initiative and my local standing were decisive in clearing their name. The story of the taxidermist did not come out and the brothers were released within the hour.

Apparently, they were eternally grateful to me. Martial, the elder brother, had been arrested two years earlier for dealing in stolen jewellery and even the smallest offence could have landed him in jail.

As we left the police station, an image was playing in my head of two powerful crowbars springing the locks on the door of my apartment. I saw it as clearly as if I were there, forcing the metal and wood to give way with a loud crack.

I had found the solution that would save my collections from the auction room.

On the pretext of going for a drive around Rivaille to help me recall the missing fragments of my past, I took out the old Santana 4x4 we use in the vineyards. After crossing the village square, I followed a back road towards the breaker's yard.

I couldn't resist making a quick detour via the 'Madman's Pond' – named after a man who tried to drown himself there eleven times before opting for the noose. I got out of the Santana and stood by the dark waters. Scanning the surface, I tried to make out the Jaguar. Nothing.

This place, which I had first spotted before I set off for Thomas l'imposteur, was where I had sunk my car. After nightfall, I had driven my coupé up to the edge of the pond, whose depth I had measured using a long stick the day before. I allowed myself a cigarette before doing for real what I had previously seen only in films: opening all the windows, taking off the handbrake, pushing the car towards the water and watching with wonder as it sank.

My Jaguar proved itself worthy of its final role; it slipped slowly under the water, its disappearance accompanied by occasional bursts of bubbles, until there was nothing left but the roof, and then nothing at all. The pond was silent again, as if nothing had ever happened. I returned to the chateau on foot, avoiding any passers-by, and claimed to have given the car back to the doctor and taken a taxi home.

Afterwards, Mélaine and I pored over Dr Baretti's file. A fine example of the genre, it was so incredibly detailed it could never be called into question. Even the police had praised the doctor's unrivalled professionalism.

'It's men like that who should be getting the Légion d'honneur!' declared Commander Briard. 'Instead they hand it out to singers and actresses, more's the pity.'

Back on the road, I followed signs towards the breaker's yard at Le Pivert. The old Santana flew through the warm summer afternoon air, and I was singing the catchy theme of *The Draughtsman's Contract* as I entered the car graveyard. I parked the Santana quite close to the entrance so that the powerful pincer manoeuvring the carcasses would not confuse it with the cars on its list for crushing that day. The redheaded man at the controls peered out of the cabin.

'Yes? Whaddaya want?' he shouted amid the din of crumpling metal.

A door opened in a little elevated workman's hut

accessed via a set of metal steps. Another man looked over at me, himself a redhead. He was in his forties, wearing a blue vest, and his low brow and little close-set eyes gave him a sheep-like air.

'Leave this to me,' he shouted at the other man. 'It's Monsieur le Comte!'

He came over and shook my hand.

'Can we help you, Monsieur le Comte?'

'I believe so,' I replied.

'Is it about the car?' he said straight away, pointing to the dusty old Santana.

'No.'

'Oh.'

'It's … a sort of favour I have to ask you.'

He nodded knowingly as if to say no further explanation was necessary.

'Martial! Get down from that thing!' he shouted up to his brother.

The pincers stopped with a clang and then swung in the air, silent and menacing. Martial came to join us and shook my hand in turn. I had before me two ginger sheep ready to do anything their shepherd asked of them.

'Fancy a beer, M'sieur le Comte?' Noël suggested.

On the table, four empty beer cans lay on the oilcloth alongside a map drawn in biro on the back of an old beige folder. I had shown them the layout of the apartment, the hallway, the living room and finally the study. They would have three hours to completely empty the room. It didn't give them much time, but they would, as they put it, 'sort it'. Neither of them asked why the Comte de Mandragore wanted to burgle an apartment in Paris. They didn't need to know.

'And the woman? What if she comes back?' Noël asked.

'She shouldn't be there. Thursday's when she goes to the hairdresser.'

This seemed to satisfy Martial, but Noël returned to the topic of Charlotte.

'If we see the woman, we'll sort her,' said Martial firmly. 'Don't worry, Monsieur le Comte. We know what we're doing.'

Afterwards we focused on the details: what kind of lock was on the door, what to expect from the neighbours, how much bubble wrap and boxes were required to pack everything, what sort of van and storage to arrange.

On the question of storage, the Davier brothers offered me the use of a shed a few kilometres away, which currently only housed 'a few bits and bobs'. The break-in was set to take place in five days' time. As the boss of the operation, I had to be available on my mobile that day, in case anything came up. The new plan I had just signed up to with France Télécom-Orange would be put to use for the first time. True professionals, the Davier brothers came up with code names for us all. I was 'Mate', they were 'Rascal' and 'Tintin', and my beloved collections, 'the Big Dog'.

That Thursday evening, I went for a walk in the rose garden before joining Mélaine for an aperitif. We were expecting the McEllies, dear friends from America passing through Burgundy; it was Arthur who had given Mélaine the rose bearing her name. Having closely followed the news of my tragic disappearance, they were overjoyed at the prospect of seeing me again. Mélaine had shown me the sympathetic notes these lovely New Yorkers had emailed from their mansion overlooking Central Park.

We had taken a picture of ourselves, cheeks pressed together, smiling into a digital camera held at arm's length, and sent it to them. 'I'm back' was my straightforward caption. The reply was not long in coming: mcellie. nyforever@aol.com: 'OH MY GOD!' were the words writ large across the screen.

I was walking on the white flagstones when my mobile rang. I picked it up straight away. I had not heard from the Davier brothers all afternoon and a dark thought was forming in my mind: I might never see my collections again. The brothers might have taken off with them, denying all knowledge when I turned up at the breaker's yard. They might even fire a few warning shots. They were crooks but I trusted them, and they seemed happy to be able to repay their debt towards me. I've always had a lot of respect for lowlifes – their brutal, no-nonsense code of honour seems to me more reliable than the morality of men in white collars.

'Hello, mate.'

It was Martial speaking.

'We've picked up your big dog. He's in his kennel. But, my God, he's heavy!'

'He didn't bark?'

This was code for asking if Charlotte had come home.

'No, he's very well behaved, that dog.'

'He didn't bump his paws or scratch his nose?'

Code for ascertaining if anything had been broken.

'Not a single bump. You can come and play ball with him whenever you like. Bye, mate.'

'Bye, Tintin, and say thanks to Rascal, too.'

'Will do.'

The next day, my collections went into the shed to which Martial Davier had given me the key.

'Keep it, Monsieur le Comte. We all have our little secrets,' he said solemnly, raising his chin as stiffly as a colonel.

What exactly had happened in Paris? Had destiny obscured my pastel so that I would be the only one to recognise myself in it?

I had often toyed with this somewhat fantastical idea. It was a compelling explanation, at once mysterious and romantic, like the pursuit which had led me to live in this chateau. I imagined that Auguste Chaumont de Rivaille had given his portrait to a shady alchemist who had performed some magic spells using mandrakes that rendered the portrait different according to who was looking at it. And yet really, of course, I knew that no such thing had occurred.

Now, I began to see the only explanation that made sense. The truth, somewhat disappointing though it was, still made my head spin. I believe that Charlotte and her lover Chevrier and our friends who came for aperitifs were all in it together. It was not that far-fetched; I think they simply wanted to play a trick on me, the lawyer who had done better than them and who spent his money so shamefully on what they regarded as dull old things.

I think that when Charlotte's gaze fell on the portrait in the living room, and I pressed her to give me her opinion of it, she saw an ideal opportunity to get back at me. 'What am I supposed to notice?' 'He looks nothing like you.' She knew that those remarks would get to me far more than quizzing me about the cost. And she was right.

I think she wanted to teach me a lesson. She was annoyed because objects that were supposed to be confined to the study had started making an appearance in the rest of the apartment, and no doubt there were one or two other things I was guilty of in her eyes. A phone message from one of her friends that I had forgotten to pass on, or a promised meal in a restaurant also forgotten, or maybe a plan for a weekend I had not followed through on. The portrait gave her the chance to exact a little revenge, and she had told Chevrier about it so that he could back her up if I showed him the portrait. She must also have warned our friends that 'Pierre-François will show you a weird portrait which does look quite like him, but whatever you do, don't let on that it does ...' They must all have been exchanging looks, and enjoying their complicity in denying the resemblance. As soon as I left the living room, disappointed, to return the picture to my study, how they must all have laughed. All my circle knew each other and they would have delighted in the little trick, whose consequences they could never have predicted.

So there was no alchemy, magic or spell. Just a petty practical joke, a mean-minded plot by embittered little people who had decided to get under the skin of the most successful member of their group. Unfortunately, I fear, it was nothing more than that.

If Charlotte had expressed astonishment the day I had shown her the portrait, if she had immediately cried, 'Where did you find that, Pierre-François, it's incredible!', if that's what she had done, nothing would have happened. And if only our friends had accepted that I was the one who had been clever by snapping up the portrait ... But they didn't want to, not any more. Deep down, they didn't like me; they had never liked me. Their attitude to the portrait had just been the conclusive proof of that.

'Go and get your picture, Pierre-François.' I can still hear her triumphant voice. That was the signal. 'Get lost' is the expression you use to someone you want to get rid of.

And I did get lost and I found myself here.

And here I still am.

The walls of the shed are wobbling in the sweltering heat, as if the metal is inflamed and swelling noisily. Inside, it's like a furnace. I get up and take a last look at my treasures in the candlelight before putting out the candles one by one with the snuffer, a little pair of silver scissors with a trap on one of the blades to catch the wick and quickly snuff out the flame. Twenty-three candles to extinguish – my visits always end this way. It's a ritual, like the cigarette and the mug of Bowmore. My mass is over and the heat is making my cheeks drip with sweat. I put the snuffer back on its stand and feel my way towards the shed's heavy door. I slide it open and I'm dazzled by the sun. It's like a decompression chamber; the shed is a little parallel universe to which I alone hold the key, a darkened room in which to commune with the departed. Pierre-François Chaumont, are you there? Knock once for yes, twice for no.

I wipe my forehead with the back of my sleeve and head towards the dirt track that leads up the hill to Rivaille. In half an hour I'll be at the chateau, in the living room on the moat side, having tea with Mélaine.

'What have you been up to?'

'Not much, just a walk,' I'll reply.

We enjoy the ritual of taking tea in this cool, slightly damp room. If you listen carefully when the windows are ajar, you can sometimes hear the slap of a carp breaking the surface before diving back down into its liquid night. Mélaine goes to the window and lifts the net curtain, her gaze lost in the dark waters, and then turns and looks at me. A knowing smile appears on her face, she drops the curtain and slowly walks towards me, step by step, never taking her eyes off me. When she reaches me, she sits down beside me, runs her hand through my hair and, as I open my mouth to speak, she places a finger on my lips. Then we look at each other without a word. At moments like this, I'm sure she knows.

She knows I'm not her husband. And I'm just as sure that we'll never speak about it. We love each other too much to risk spoiling our happiness by bringing up what is, after all, a minor detail.

A thud like the fall of a meteorite wrapped in cotton wool rings out behind me and I freeze. Suddenly I feel dizzy and the hot trails of sweat glistening on my forehead turn ice-cold. I know what this noise, this thud is. There's nothing else it could be.

I try to catch my breath, gritting my teeth, as the

first creaking sounds come from the metal walls. I can't move; it's as if my legs are welded to the ground. All at once a rising crackling sound can be heard on the warm breeze, followed by more pops and bangs like firecrackers. They're coming from the old ammunition crate that was left near the sacks of fertiliser. I'm rooted to the spot. My mind is entirely blank. I am already in the moat-side living room drinking tea with Mélaine. I'm looking at her; my gaze glides over the white cotton dress she was wearing this morning and then back up to her hair. I see her body and feel her presence so strongly it's surreal. Now that I've understood what went on in Paris, something must happen. Now that I've found the woman, the love and the beauty I spent so long searching for in objects as I built up my collections, now that I've passed from the inanimate to the living, a strange kind of transaction must take place, like paying a smuggler a fortune to cross a forbidden frontier: every object I own, for a single woman.

It's the price I have to pay. The cost of happiness.

At last I find the strength to turn around. Just then, the roof of the shed caves in and a blast of scorching air and ash hits me in the face and rushes through my hair. I close my eyes.

'Pierre-François Chaumont, are you there? Knock once for yes, twice for no.'

Two cartridges explode in reply, one after the other, loud and clear.

Reading Group Discussion Points:

• What significance do inanimate objects have for Pierre-François Chaumont? How do you interpret the eventual fate of his collection?

• Antoine Laurain's characters often undergo a transformation which allows them to start their lives afresh. To what extent is he an optimistic writer?

• *Le Figaro* said of Laurain's last novel, *French Rhapsody*: 'What makes it one of the must-reads of the moment is not just its off-the-wall humour, but its deep sense of melancholy. If it wasn't so funny, you'd weep for the roads not taken.' How does Antoine Laurain balance humour and melancholy in *The Portrait*?

• To what extent can *The Portrait* be read as a fable, and the painting as having magical properties?

• Does Pierre-François behave in a morally acceptable way, in your opinion? What about Charlotte and Mélaine?

• To what extent is *The Portrait* about identity, the way we see and present ourselves and the way others perceive us?

• *The Portrait* was Antoine Laurain's first novel, written while he was working for an antiques dealer. What themes from this book carry on into his later novels?

The President's Hat
Antoine Laurain
translated by Gallic Books

Dining alone in an elegant Parisian brasserie, accountant
Daniel Mercier can hardly believe his eyes when
President François Mitterrand sits down to eat at the table
next to him.

After the presidential party has gone, Daniel discovers
that Mitterrand's black felt hat has been left behind. After
a few moments' soul-searching, Daniel decides to keep
the hat as a souvenir of an extraordinary evening. It's a
perfect fit, and as he leaves the restaurant Daniel begins
to feel somehow … different.

ISBN: 9781908313478
e-ISBN: 9781908313577

The Red Notebook
Antoine Laurain
translated by Emily Boyce and Jane Aitken

Bookseller Laurent Letellier comes across an abandoned
handbag on a Parisian street, and feels impelled to
return it to its owner.

The bag contains no money, phone or contact
information. But a small red notebook with handwritten
thoughts and jottings reveals a person that Laurent would
very much like to meet.

Without even a name to go on, and only a few of her
possessions to help him, how is he to find one woman in a
city of millions?

ISBN: 9781908313867
e-ISBN: 9781908313874

French Rhapsody
Antoine Laurain
translated by Emily Boyce and Jane Aitken

Middle-aged doctor Alain Massoulier has received a life-changing letter – thirty-three years too late.

Lost in the Paris postal system for decades, the letter from Polydor, dated 1983, offers a recording contract to The Holograms, in which Alain played lead guitar.

Overcome by nostalgia, Alain is tempted to track down the members of the group. But in a world where everything and everyone has changed … where could his quest possibly take him?

ISBN: 9781910477304
e-ISBN: 9781910477380

An extract from

French Rhapsody

A Letter

The assistant manager, a tired-looking little man with a narrow, greying moustache, had invited him to sit down in a tiny windowless office brightened only by its canary-yellow door. When Alain saw the carefully framed notice, he felt nervous laughter return – but more hysterical this time, and accompanied by the disagreeable feeling that if God existed, he had a very dubious sense of humour. The notice showed a joyful team of postmen and -women all giving the thumbs up. Running across the top in yellow letters were the words 'The future: brought to you by the Post Office.' Alain chuckled mirthlessly. 'Great slogan.'

'No need to be sarcastic, Monsieur,' replied the civil servant calmly.

'Don't you think I'm entitled to a little sarcasm?' demanded Alain, pointing to his letter. 'Thirty-three years late. How do you explain that?'

'Your tone is not helpful, Monsieur,' replied the man drily.

Alain glared at him. The assistant manager held his gaze for a moment, then slowly extended his arm towards a blue folder which he opened with some ceremony. Then he licked his finger and started turning the pages, rather slowly. 'And your name is?' he murmured, not looking at Alain.

'Massoulier,' replied Alain.

'Ah, yes, Dr Alain Massoulier, 38 Rue de Moscou, Paris 8^e,' the civil servant read aloud. 'You're aware that we're modernising?'

'The results are impressive.'

The man with the moustache looked at Alain again in silence and seemed about to say something sharp, but apparently thought better of it.

'As I was saying, the building is being modernised, so all the wooden shelves, dating back to its construction in 1954, were taken down last week. The workmen found four letters which had fallen down the back and were trapped between the floor and the shelves. The oldest dated back to … 1963,' he confirmed, reading from the file. 'Then there was a postcard from 1978, a letter from 1983 – that's yours – and lastly, a letter from 2002. We took the decision that, where possible, we would deliver them to their recipients if they were still alive and easily identifiable from their addresses. That's the explanation,' he said, closing the blue file.

'But no apology?' said Alain.

Eventually the assistant manager said, 'If you wish, we can send you our apology form letter. Would that be of use?'

Alain looked down at the desk where his eye fell on a heavy cast-iron paperweight, embellished with the insignia of the postal service. He briefly saw himself picking it up and hitting the little moustachioed man with it repeatedly.

'For whatever purpose it may serve,' droned the man, 'does this letter have a legal significance (with regard to an inheritance or transfer of shares or similar) such that the delay in delivery would activate legal proceedings against the postal service—'

'No, it does not,' Alain cut him off brusquely.

The man asked him for his signature at the bottom of a form that Alain did not even bother to read. Alain left and stopped outside in front of a skip. Workmen were throwing solid oak planks and metal structures into it, shouting at each other in what Alain believed was Serbian.

Passing a mirror in a chemist's window, Alain caught sight of his reflection. He saw grey hair and the rimless glasses that his optician claimed were as good as a facelift. An ageing doctor, that's what the mirror reflected back at him, an ageing doctor like so many thousands of others across the country. A doctor, just like his father before him.

Written on a typewriter and signed in turquoise ink, the letter had arrived in the morning post. In the top left-hand corner was the logo of the famous record label: a semicircle above the name, featuring a vinyl record in the form of a setting sun – or maybe a rising sun. The paper had yellowed at the edges. Alain had reread the letter three times before putting it back in the envelope. His name was correct, his address was correct. Everything was in order except for the date, 12 September 1983. That date was also printed over the stamp – a Marianne that had been out of circulation for a long time. The postmark was only half printed but you could clearly read: Paris – 12/9/83. Alain had suppressed a fleeting guffaw like an unwelcome tic. Then he had shaken his head, smiling incredulously. Thirty-three years. That letter had taken thirty-three years to travel across three *arrondissements* of the capital.

The day's post – an electricity bill, *Le Figaro*, *L'Obs,* three publicity flyers (one for a mobile phone, one for a travel agent and the third for an insurance company) – had just been brought up by Madame Da Silva, the concierge. Alain had considered getting up, opening the door and catching Madame Da Silva on the stairs to ask her where the letter had come from. But she would already be back downstairs in her apartment, and anyway, she wouldn't be able to help him. She had merely brought up what the postman had delivered to the building.

Paris, 12 September 1983

Dear Holograms

We listened with great interest to the five-track demo tape you sent us at the beginning of the summer. Your work is precise and very professional, and although it needs quite a bit of work, you already have a sound that is distinctive. The track we were most impressed by was 'Such Stuff as Dreams Are Made On'. You have managed to blend new wave and cold wave whilst adding your own rock sound.

Please get in touch with us so that we can organise a meeting.

Best wishes

Claude Kalan
ARTISTIC DIRECTOR

The tone was polite but friendly. Alain focused on the words 'precise' and 'very professional' whilst noting the slightly derogatory repetition of the word 'work'. And the letter ended on an encouraging note, an affirmation in fact. Yes, thought Alain, 'Such Stuff as Dreams Are Made On' was the best, a jewel, a hit, whispered in Bérengère's voice. Alain closed his eyes and recalled her face with almost surreal precision: her big eyes, always vaguely worried, her short haircut with the fringe sweeping over her forehead, the way she had of going up to the mic and holding it with both hands and not letting go for the whole song. She would close her eyes and the soft voice with its touch of huskiness was always a surprise coming from a girl of nineteen. Alain opened his eyes again: 'a meeting' – how many times had the five of them uttered that word. How many times had they hoped for a meeting with a record label: a meeting at eleven on Monday at our offices. We have a meeting at Polydor. That 'meeting' had never been forthcoming. The Holograms had split up. Although that was not exactly the right term. It would be more accurate to say that life had simply moved on, causing the group to disperse. In the absence of a response from any record label, they had each gone their own way, disappointed and tired of waiting.

Still half asleep in her blue silk dressing gown, Véronique had just pushed open the kitchen door. Alain looked up at her and handed her the letter. She read it through, yawning.

'It's a mistake,' she said.

'It certainly is not,' retorted Alain, holding out the envelope. 'Alain Massoulier, that's me.'

'I don't understand.' Véronique shook her head, indicating that untangling an enigma so soon after waking up was beyond her.

'The date, look at the date.'

She read out, '1983.'

'The Holograms, that was my group, my rock group. Well, it wasn't rock, it was new wave; cold wave to be exact, as it says here.' Alain pointed to the relevant line in the letter.

Véronique looked at her husband in astonishment.

'The letter took thirty-three years to travel across three *arrondissements*.'

'Are you sure?' she murmured, turning the letter over.

'Have you got another explanation?'

'You'll have to ask at the post office,' concluded Véronique, sitting down.

'I'm going to! I wouldn't miss that for the world,' replied Alain.

Then he got up and started the Nespresso machine.

'Make me one,' said Véronique, yawning again.

Alain thought it was time his wife cut down on the sleeping tablets. It was distressing to see her every morning appearing like a rumpled shrew. It would take her at least two hours in the bathroom before she emerged dressed and made up. So all in all it took nearly three hours for Véronique to get herself properly together. Since the children had left home, Alain and Véronique found themselves living on their own as at the beginning of their marriage. But twenty-five years had passed and what had seemed charming at the beginning was becoming a little wearing, and now long silences stretched out over dinner. In order to fill them Véronique talked about her clients and her latest decorative finds, while Alain would mention patients or colleagues, and then they would fall to discussing their holiday plans although they could never agree where to go.